Earth and Luna were bright demidisks against black space, a sight no one had seen for 780 New Home years. Nikko was surprised at her emotions; it was as if she was coming home. "They're beautiful, Ram," she said, "just beautiful."

But treachery, not beauty, had greeted them on landing. "Captain," said Draco into the captured radio, "all I ask as ransom is your other sky chariot with all your guns and grenades."

Ram's voice was thick with suppressed anger. "You already have the *Alpha*. If I give *Beta* to you, I can't land to pick my people up."

Draco savored the man's dilemma. "If you do not deliver it, Captain, you will have no one to pick up." He chuckled. "You must trust me."

Clearly, Ram Uithoudt needed allies—allies with strength and cunning. **Nils Järnhann's** neovikings qualified, but Ram didn't trust them either; they were violent and had their own purposes. Fortunately, Nils was good at reconciling different goals, but things could get pretty messy along the way.

John Dalmas
Homecoming

TOR

A TOM DOHERTY ASSOCIATES BOOK

HOMECOMING

First printing: September 1984

A TOR Book

Published by:
Tom Doherty Associates
8-10 West 36 Street
New York, N.Y. 10018

Cover art by: James Gurney

ISBN: 0-812-53471-9
CAN. ED.: 0-812-53472-7

Printed in the United States of America

To POUL ANDERSON, master wordsmith, master storysmith, whose people make his stories truly special.

Long odds aren't a certainty, they are a judgment. And while they can become a self-fulfilling prophecy, the very fact of odds implies that the favorite may be upset. Especially if the underdog's skill and decision pull in help—from a paranoid bystander, for example, or a pregnant witch.

I

Nikko Kumalo seldom saw the bridge on night watch, and its beauty affected her. It was "night" now by the ship's chronometer and their own circadian rhythms, and all passageway lights were muted accordingly. The bridge itself was lit mainly by the cool luminescent characters on the black computer screen and dim blue night lights in the bulkheads, with an overall effect of soft velvet. Ram had cut off the unobtrusive wake tone that kept the bridge watch alert in the dimness, and it seemed to Nikko that to speak would break a spell.

On the viewscreen were two other lights, gibbous demi-discs bright and prominent against a backdrop of black space. Her eyes fixed on them and she knew what they were.

Ram spoke quietly. "You said to call you."

"They're beautiful, Ram, just beautiful."

Her husband Matthew, standing beside her, said nothing, just looked at Earth and its satellite. After more than seven centuries, men from New Home were looking at the planet from which their ancestors had come. Back in normal space after weeks in jump phase, they could measure her distance in millions of kilometers instead of parsecs.

He shivered. What would they find there? Something drastic had happened—must have happened—long ago to have ended without warning all traffic between the mother planet and her then still infant primary colony. Blue and white showed on the screen—there were still seas and clouds. Perhaps a virulent disease or transstellar conquerors were waiting for them, as the geophobes back home had feared. Right now, he thought, we know no more than when we raised ship, except that Earth is still here, still blue and white in space. Later today we'll begin to find out other things.

So many generations had lived and died since his many-times removed great grandparents had left Earth that he hadn't expected to feel this much emotion. Briefly in the muted darkness, all four stared at the viewscreen, Nikko and Matthew hand in hand, Ram and the computerman in their duty seats, seeing what men from New Home had seen only in their imaginations since the last ship from Earth had left it 780 New Home years before.

The culture of New Home was basically agrarian, and its people in general were calm and methodical. So planetary analyses waited until general duty hours to begin. The analyses were much the same as those made by the ancient charting ships—the *Copernicus*, *Galileo*, and *Kepler*. But this time they were not being made routinely, impersonally, of new and unknown planets. The subject was the mother planet, Earth. Spectral readings indicated a planetary temperature approximately two and a half Celsius degrees below twenty-first century levels. The absorption spectrum indicated no significant change in atmospheric CO_2, and a reduction in water vapor compatible with the temperature change. Albedo seemed high, suggesting greater than old-normal cloud cover, but the existing level was not outside the limits of twenty-first century variability.

What everyone was really waiting for were exploration flights within the atmosphere. It was the northern hemisphere spring—the computer said May 24 by the Gregorian calendar—and as the shadow of night moved out over the eastern Atlantic, the *Phaeacia* began a close survey pattern 900 kilometers above sea level. Carefully she scanned for the radiation signatures of cities. And found none.

Pinnace *Alpha* launched at ship's midday and began scouting the sunlit Americas from within the troposphere. She sighted villages reminiscent of early American Indian villages, in openings seemingly cleared by fire. Baby ice sheets glistened whitely in Keewatin, the Ungava Peninsula, and the Canadian Rockies, and forests covered the eastern half of North America from the Gulf of Mexico to north of Lake Superior.

In 2100 A.D. there had been more than 1.47 billion people in the western hemisphere. Matthew Kumalo radioed that there would hardly be more than five or ten million now.

"Duty days" yielded in part to the dictates of the solar day on Earth. Low-level flights followed the sunrise into eastern Asia and across the Eurasian land mass; its ancient cities were rubble or less, many grown over with forests. There were no new cities; there were only pretechnology towns.

After several days the exploration team decided on Contact Prime—the town where first contact would be made with the people of Earth. It stood beside the old Danube ship canal, a short distance from the Black Sea. Single-masted ships lay in its harbor. Though not the largest of the new towns—it was four kilometers across—it seemed clearly the most advanced. Most towns looked like something from the Middle Ages: haphazard, ugly, and surrounded by hostile stone bastions. This town, by contrast, was rigorously geometrical, with a harmonious kind of severe beauty, an angular regularity that demonstrated the existence there of mathematicians and planners. And unfortified. Its stadium would accommodate tens of thousands, Matthew thought. A tall black tower rose from a palace with terraced roof gardens, the most impressive structure they had seen either here or at home.

Whatever had happened to mankind on Earth, Matthew thought to himself, it was rising with a new civilization. He felt cautiously eager to visit Contact Prime, to begin learning what had happened, and what was happening now.

II

Something was making the cattle restless. Their normal foraging movements had stopped, their heads raised to stare southward. It had started a moment earlier with some old cows at the south edge of the herd, and spread. He stood in his stirrups, old calves sinewy, strong bare toes supporting his wiry weight, to scan the irregular sea of grass in that direction. Perhaps wolves were moving down the draw from the forested ridge a kilometer away, hoping to take a new calf from the fringe of the herd.

Casually he took his short bow from its boot and strung it. There was no cause for concern. Last year's grass had been broken and flattened by winter snows, and the new grass was still young spears not long enough to conceal a hare. They could not move out of the draw without becoming targets for himself and the others.

It did not occur to him to think beyond wolves. But it was men who rode out of the pines, and he sat back, watching them. Horse barbarians, he thought, predatory and wild, but constrained by their fealty to the Master from attacking his herds or his herdsmen. Horse barbarians. They were of different tribes and tongues, from as near as the Southern Desert and as far as the Great Eastern Mountains, wherever those might be. But he hadn't seen any like these before. His keen eyes took in details. These were large men, some with yellow hair, and they carried no lances.

They separated, moving casually as if to encircle or half encircle the herd, and he started toward them to warn them away. They began to shout, to drive the cattle, and he called angrily at them, shaking his bow. One of the nearest raised his own bow and the herdsman stared for a shocked moment before slumping to the ground, his callused toes losing their grip on the stirrups.

The other herdsmen fled, and the intruders made no effort to stop them. They simply drove the herd across the arm of prairie toward the mountains rising to the northwest.

III

Space is deep and beautiful,
ruthless but predictable,
Inhuman.
The men of Earth
are only some of these.

From—EARTH, by Chandra Queiros

Han var Ahmed, son t' Ahmed,
han var säd a Kassis spihunn
i Kyng Janos hov på Pestad.
Svarthud var han likså faren,
långsynt åsa som d' älren,
slug å kall i pann som faren.
Läste ikke tankar tväätom,
såg han aj i själ som faren,
fäsen tävelte om makten
i d' sajkarl hövdingringen.
Ikke fegling som d' älren,
dolte aj i prysi jömme,
kjämpe han, jääv likså vasam,
hövding han blann orkahodern.

        *   *   *

Hätte rival, luden Drekå,
han som gläde sej i törtyr,
själson t' d' aset Kassi.

[Ahmed was he, son of Ahmed,
was the seed of Kazi's spy-dog
in the Magyar court of Janos.
Black-skinned was he like his father,
patient also like the elder,
ruthless, cunning, as his sire was.
Was no telepath however,
read not minds as had his father,
though he strove to rule the psi men.
Was no coward like his father
skulking in a velvet covert,
was a warrior hard and wary,
was a chieftain in the orc horde.

Had a rival, hairy Draco,
he whose pleasures lie in tortures,
Draco, soul-child of dead Kazi.]

From—THE JÄRNHANN SAGA,
Kumalo translation.

The buckled lattice of leather straps reached high
on the ankles, as on Roman sandals. The leather
soles were needlessly thick and hard, however, and
noisy with metal bosses and heel plates. They clattered harshly in the stone corridor, driven by five
pairs of strong purposeful bare legs, and turned a
blind corner without caution. Two slaves, warned
by the unsynchronized tattoo, already stood clear
with their backs to the wall. It was basic to re-

main unnoticed, and their minds were carefully blank as the officers passed, erect, hard, and arrogant.

The man who strode at the front of the group was clearly in command. One of the others, despite the pace and hard decisiveness of their march, tried to speak confidentially into the leader's ear but was cut off with a brusque gesture. The chamber they entered had no door to be opened. The corridor simply ended in it, with glass doors opposite standing open on a sun-lit balcony. Unlike the corridor, the chamber was not walled with dark polished basalt, but veneered with marble, hung with rich indigo fabric, and carpeted with furs.

Five men awaited the five, and they too had an obvious leader. All ten dressed much the same: boots, short-sleeved tunic, and light harness with an ornamental breast plate, silver for the leaders, polished bronze for the others. Their visible weapons were short swords, ceremonial but also lethal.

The waiting leader, Draco, was Mediterranean in appearance, ugly-handsome, with olive skin, thick close-cropped curly hair, and a mat resembling black fur curling on his forearms and bare legs. He looked like a compact gladiator, mean and muscular, brutal and deadly.

The leader of the second five, Ahmed, was taller and more slender—fine-boned, actually—giving somehow the simultaneous impressions of smoothness and lean muscularity. His coloring was coffee brown, his hair a skullcap of fine kinks. He was cool, contained, and calculating, and the impression of deadliness he gave was different than Draco's—if there was gloating to be done it would follow, not anticipate the act.

"Your men are the garrison force," Ahmed opened coldly. "You clean them out. If you can."

Draco smirked. "The region north and west of the Danube is your responsibility. The Master himself assigned the sectors." He stared amusedly at Ahmed, the tilt of his head suggesting that he, the telepath, was listening to more than the Sudanese wanted to tell him.

Ahmed knew better. To him, screening was no effort; it was just there. Words came to his dark lips and action to the slender-strong fingers with seeming spontaneity. Only that effortless screening enabled him to compete successfully with ruthless telepaths for leadership.

"Have you forgotten his final instructions to you?" Ahmed replied. "Let me quote them. 'Draco, I know you have the taste and wits for the job, and I am leaving you plenty of men. I also know you're lazy, careless, and inclined to overkill when left alone. Do not forget, while I am gone, that I will return. When I do, everything must be in order. *I hold you responsible* for any revolts, *or incursions by wandering tribes*. Also keep in mind that dead slaves are of no further use except to the commissary department, and beef is much cheaper.'"

It was a remarkably close quote, delivered with the same contemptuous condescension as the original. Only the emphases were Ahmed's. And the quotation carried a background, a context not apparent in the words themselves. Both of Kazi's lieutenants, bitter antagonists, had wanted field command in the Russian campaign, and Ahmed had been chosen.

Draco's face darkened with anger. "*But he did not come back. His field commander led the army to defeat and allowed the Master to be killed.* Now the situation is different. I am my own master and make my own decisions. I have no more responsibility north of the Danube."

Ahmed smiled slightly. "This city is north of the Danube. Do I command it alone then?"

Draco's eyes bulged with sudden anger, his left hand clutching reflexively at his hilt. "We are *south* of it!" he snarled. "Are you completely ignorant? The City is north of the canal but south of the Danube!"

"A quibble. The Master treated the canal as the eastward extension of the river." Ahmed's tone became more reasonable now, almost conciliatory. "Besides, my defeat you remind me of left only a ragged few hundred of their warriors alive. Not every Northman is a warrior; not even most of them. The great majority are peasants. Consider then that my army did its part when we butchered so many of them in the Ukraine. We have paid our share of the cost. And you do not want it said that Draco preferred to leave the fighting to others."

Draco did consider, screening from the psis on Ahmed's staff. Perhaps this was an opportunity. Ahmed had failed in the Ukraine, but he had not been an experienced field commander; his position had come from his father's influence with Kazi. While he, Draco, had risen through the ranks.

His patrols had several times encountered Northman patrols and raiding parties with results ranging from exasperating to shocking. But those had been chance engagements, not part of a systematic campaign. And the Northmen were no longer a free-roving war party, vulnerable only in their persons. Their whole nation was with them now, peasants, women and children, making them a much easier nut to crack. If he destroyed them he would be recognized as the new Master.

"I'll think about it," he answered stiffly. Ahmed would not have set this before him without having trouble or treachery in mind, but that he could handle when the time came.

Ahmed relaxed alone in his windowless chamber, its thick stone walls effectively shielding his thoughts. Draco had taken the bait. Like tough meat, the Northmen would take forever to chew up. And Draco was unstable: the frustration would destroy his judgment. He would undoubtedly eliminate the Northmen as a problem, but by then his army would be reduced and demoralized and his prestige broken.

IV

Pinnace *Alpha* was by no means the most sophisticated craft ever built. New Home had inherited the technical and scientific knowledge of late twenty-first century Earth, much of it, stored in books and tapes. But her culture was agrarian and her high tech industry non-existent, whether cybernetics, inframolecular, biosynthetics, or electronics. Sophisticated components couldn't be ordered from a contractor; there were no contractors. They were handcrafted in the shop or the lab, or done without. It hadn't even been possible to go out and buy much of the requisite shop and lab equipment; they'd had to be handcrafted too.

But she was easy to fly.

Now *Alpha* coasted downward through the ionosphere along a gravitic vector extending through Contact Prime, the AG coils generating only enough to hold acceleration within safe limits. As they approached the F1 layer, Matthew eased in the accumulator, slowing for entry and continuing to decelerate. Soon they were no longer approaching a planet; they seemed instead to be above the ground and dropping downward.

At four kilometers above the city Matthew slowed and began spiraling toward it in broad loops.

"I almost said that's a handsome city," said Nikko Kumalo, "but I think impressive's the better word."

"I'd go for both," said Mikhail Ciano. "Whoever built it was a damned good engineer."

At two hundred meters they leveled off and circled, and Matthew switched the hull to one-way transparent. Below they could see growing clusters of people staring upward toward them. He fingered a dial beneath the viewscreen and a group on a rooftop snapped into large magnification.

He whistled silently. "What do you think of that?"

"Soldiers!" said Chandra Queiros.

Matthew shifted the view from place to place; soldiers were present or even prominent almost everywhere, straight-backed and hard-faced. Mikhail Ciano watched thoughtfully. "They look like Roman legionaries. I'll bet I know now why this city isn't walled. They're not only the best engineers and organizers around; they've probably got the best army."

Matthew pursed his lips and nodded thoughtfully, then slid the pinnace into a climbing northwesterly course, leveling off at a thousand meters.

"What is it, Matt?" asked Anne Marie Queiros. "Why are we leaving?"

"I'm not ready to make real contact yet. We've given them a look at us—given them something to think and talk about. That'll be enough for now."

He looked back at the others. "We're not prepared yet, psychologically, to deal with what looks like a military society. At least I'm not. I need to digest what we saw back there. Back home we've had seven centuries of peace and relative sanity; we haven't had dealings with foreign cultures of any kind. Our responses aren't conditioned to people like those back there."

He looked ahead again at the broad grassland across which they flew. "Besides, there's no hurry. I want more data, and some time to think about it."

"There's one thing I'll bet I already know about them," Chandra said.

"What's that?"

"They didn't built that city with heavy equipment. They built it with slaves."

For a while they flew without further talk. "How far have we come?" Nikko asked after a bit.

"From the city? A hundred and forty-one kilometers."

"We haven't seen so much as a village in the whole distance. Nothing more than a few tent camps near the cattle herds."

"Well there's something over there," Mikhail said pointing. "About three hundred degrees from course azimuth."

They peered at a low cloud of distant dust, then Matthew turned the craft in a broad arc, climbing as he did so. Mikhail targeted the viewscreen and set it on automatic hold. In a little more than a minute they were hovering at 4,500 meters, too high to be noticed when motionless.

From there they watched two mounted companies approach each other a little distance apart; Nikko reactivated the camera. Abruptly both sides broke into a gallop, and Mikhail increased magnification. The smaller troop, of perhaps thirty men, rode in a near-perfect line with lances raised. The other line was ragged, its riders lanceless, and a flight of arrows coursed from it, and another. Lancers and horses began to fall, and their ranks closed to fill the holes. Then the bowmen's line fragmented, its riders veering in pairs to the sides, drawing swords, forcing the lancers to slow and turn, losing the momentum that made their lances effective. Some lances dipped to strike regardless while others were dropped in favor.of swords, and Mikhail raised the magnification again. Horses and men milled in concentrated violence amid billowing tawny dust, striking, colliding, falling.

They watched with shocked fascination. In moments the surviving lancers broke away to flee. Bowmen pursued them, loosing arrows. Three lancers dropped from their horses. Six horses fell, tumbling their riders. None escaped. The bowmen rode near the unhorsed, stopped casually to take aim, then shot them and dismounted. Mike zoomed the lens to full magnification. Even through the resultant image waver they could see the grins as the victors scalped the fallen. Shifting the focus showed other scalpings at the battle site nearby.

"Talk about savages," Chandra whispered.

"Let's break out the automatic rifles and run them off," Mikhail suggested. "Maybe shoot a few of their horses to give them the idea."

"No." Matthew's voice was thoughtful but positive, and he tilted the pinnace in a descending spiral. "We don't know which side are the good guys yet." Shortly they hovered only twenty meters above the grass, at an oblique angle convenient for viewing through the craft's side. The scalpers had stopped, standing erect to watch the pinnace, and a glance at the viewscreen showed their magnified faces narrow-eyed, intent, without apparent fear. They were strong-necked and hard-faced, wearing braids and short beards, their shoulders heavy in mail shirts, thighs powerful in soft leather breeches. After a few still moments followed by some verbal exchange, one unslung his bow, strung it, and fired at the *Alpha* while the others watched.

On board they could hear the faint rap as the arrow struck. "Incredible!" Chandra breathed. "They're insane!" After a short pause, other raps sounded. Then the bowmen gathered, talking with frequent glances upward. Most mounted and sat with an eye on the pinnace while several still on foot moved about working efficiently with their knives. Then they too mounted, and all fanned out to collect the loitering horses of the fallen of both sides. Slender ropes uncoiled, and when they rode away, with occasional backward looks, a number of them had a spare horse trailing.

Matthew lifted and they quickly climbed out of sight to six kilometers, watching the viewscreen.

"Total savages," Chandra said. "I can hardly believe there are actually human beings like that."

"Also totally efficient," Mikhail replied drily, "and we'd better believe it." He turned to Matthew. "What was it old Gus Fong said? We'd bring back stories that would change the world."

"Something like that." Matthew read the polar azimuth of the barbarians' course and moved ahead of them in that direction far above their view. Forest-dark mountains drew near, moved beneath, and pinnace *Alpha* slowed to a near hover. His deliberate hands manipulated and the landscape below slid smoothly across the viewscreen, magnification low as he transected the terrain. Within three minutes he found what he sought, a long grassy valley between forested ridges, with clusters of rude huts strung out for several kilometers. He dropped slowly, zooming the pickup for close examinations, retracting it for perspective.

The people's identity seemed unquestionable. Like the warriors, many were light-haired, though most were not so strongly built. Women carried water and wood. Children helped or followed them or played and wrestled. Men and youths tended cattle from horseback, speared fish in the stream or swam in its pools. Others shot at marks, and many, on foot and on horseback, trained with swords.

Matthew read their position to the servo-mech, then instructed it to locate the homing beam and return to the *Phaeacia*. As they started their rendezvous trajectory he sat back pensively.

"What are you thinking about?" Chandra asked him.

Matthew tugged thoughtfully at his chin. "The barbarians. They look temporary, like a people in migration. No garden patches, nothing permanent looking ... I wonder if they know what they're getting into?"

"I see what you mean," Mikhail said. "They're badly outnumbered and outclassed, regardless of how tough they might be."

"Right. I'd say the fight we saw was something like attacking a dire bear with a stick; you might get in the first blow or two, but then good night! If I was one of those people down there I'd load my family and gear on my horses and start putting distance between me and that city."

V

Fanns allri nannan som Ynglingen han—
milt som mjök (önar leene),
stark som storm (men allri raste),
vis som jodens sälva ännen.

Å varelse var han, aj dykt.

[There was never other like the Youngling,
mild as milk (his eyes smiling),
strong as storm (but never raging),
wise as the spirit of the earth.

And living man he was, not myth.]

Prefatory verse of THE JÄRNHANN SAGA,
Kumalo translation

The long low ridge extended eastward from the
foothills a considerable distance into the open plain.
Its cool north-facing slope was green with new
grass. At intervals, shallow draws ran down it,
thick with low shrubby oaks whose soft, late-
emerging leaflets tinted their gray with pink. Along

20

the crest, broken rock let rain and melting snow penetrate deeply; and a ragged line of scraggly shrubs grew there, overlooking a semi-barren south slope.

The sky was cloudless and immense, the sun warm. Gnats hung in the air, celebrating the absence of wind, and an eagle soared, tilting and swaying in the updrafts. A mouse scurried between two spiny shrubs and a sparrow hawk darted toward it, rising again with the furry victim in its small talons.

The two adolescents, prone within the screen of shrubs, watched the brief tiny drama with sharp eyes, then looked southward across the plain again. Sweat oiled their dirty foreheads. Gnats hovered and bit unheeded. After several minutes the younger said softly, "There is something else I like about this country; you can see so far."

The other nodded curtly, and for a time they said nothing, did nothing except scan the plain.

"Look," the younger spoke again, and pointed southward.

"Jaha. Men on horseback; it looks like three."

They watched awhile. "There is one trotting ahead on foot," the older added. "About a hundred meters ahead."

The other squinted. "I see him. It looks as if they plan to cross the ridge over east, where it isn't so steep."

They crawled back from the crest, then ran downslope to their horses tethered to a clump of oak shrubs. Untying them, they scrambled to their backs and started eastward at a gallop. A kilometer farther they angled up the slope and tied their horses again, then ran toward the crest, wriggling the last few meters on their bellies to lie panting among some shrubs.

They were startled to see how near the running man was, perhaps seventy meters off. He stopped.

"He's looking at us!" hissed the younger. "How can he see us?"

The man raised his hand, halting the others— two men and a woman.

"They are our people!" the younger added.

"I can see that!" the older whispered with irritation.

The warrior started diagonally up the slope toward them, trotting easily. They could see as he came how big he was, an agile giant, shirtless, glistening, thick muscles moving smoothly in torso and limbs.

"It's the Yngling!" the younger whispered.

"You don't know; you never saw him."

They stayed on their stomachs, eyes large, until their necks were craned backward and the man stood above them. Sweat dripped from his nose and trickled down his grimy torso. Strong teeth showed between the long sparse tow-colored mustache and an even sparser growth on his chin.

"Just what we need," he said. "Someone to guide us to the People."

Both boys got up.

"You *are* the Yngling, aren't you?" asked the younger.

"Some say so," the man said grinning. "I am Nils Järnhann, warrior of the Wolf Clan, of the Svear. And you are lookouts. Where are your horses?"

The older boy pointed. "But one of us must stay

here on watch. I am the oldest, so I will stay. Alvar will guide you."

Nils nodded and gestured for the others. "Fine. What is your name?"

The boy stood straight. "Ola Gulleson, sword apprentice of the Reindeer Clan of the Svear."

They shook hands and then parted, Nils and Alvar walking toward Alvar's tethered horse. "I am Ola's brother," Alvar volunteered. "He will be sixteen when the leaves fall, and I was fourteen when the snow was melting. I am a sword apprentice too."

"Good."

"You think I'm too skinny to be a sword apprentice, but things are different than they used to be. Lots of things changed this winter. And I am growing." He untied his horse. "Do you want to ride him? I can walk. Many people say we young don't want to do anything but ride. They say if we aren't careful we will be weak-legged like the horse barbarians who can walk only a short way before they are tired out. I don't want to be weak-legged. Is that why you were running? So your legs won't lose their strength?"

"I was running because we have only three horses," Nils answered matter-of-factly. "And as you say, it's good to run. When we fought the orcs in the battle of the neck, we won despite their numbers because they tired."

"You ride now," the boy said decisively. "It will be my turn to run."

The others rode up to them and the boy loped off. "The runner is also the scout," Nils called after him, "so keep your eyes and ears open."

Nils let Alvar jog some five kilometers, then called

for him to wait. "I think we can do without a scout now, and I need answers to some questions. You can share Miska's back with Ilse while we talk."

As soon as he was aboard, the boy asked, "Where did you get such fine horses?"

"From the Magyars."

"Did you steal them?"

"They gave them to us. I have friends among the Magyars; I was a soldier in their royal guard once. We wintered with them."

"Why didn't they give you four horses so you all could ride?"

Sten and Leif laughed aloud at the way the boy controlled the conversation, but that didn't faze Alvar.

"There were five of us then," Nils explained, "and they gave us ten horses, but bandits attacked us in the mountains and when they fled we were only four, with three horses."

"And now a question for you: How did the People winter?"

"The clans wintered separately, to get enough food. They were in many places in the South Ukraine. The Reindeer Clan was at a place called Kishinev. There had been villages but the orcs had burned them." Alvar paused to make a face of disgust. "House burners and barn burners! They have no shame. And they'd killed most of the people. The ones that were left had made little huts in the forest, and that's what we did too. All their warriors were dead or gone away, and the orcs had taken most of their cattle, but some had been hidden in the forest so there still were some for us to take. The Ukrainians would come and beg for food.

"After we made camp there, the Council of Chiefs

decided that *all* men must train to fight because we had too few warriors; so many had been killed, you know. And we needed to practice fighting from horseback because we were not skilled at it. And all boys from thirteen to sixteen were made sword apprentices unless something was wrong with them. We trained as hard as the hunger would let us. I'll let you feel my muscle sometime. Here." He tapped Ilse on the shoulder and doubled his right arm. "You feel it."

She turned in the saddle—awkwardly, for she was eight months pregnant—and squeezed his bicep. "It isn't very big yet," she said, "but it is hard as a rock."

Alvar blushed. "You talk funny," he said. "You are not of the People. Even the Sydnorskar talk better than that."

"True," Ilse said. "I am Deuts, and I've only been learning your tongue since last fall. But now I also am one of the People because Nils is, and I am his wife."

They rode without talking for a bit, but shortly Alvar asked: "Are you a thought reader, like Nils, that can look into People's minds?"

"Yes."

Alvar blushed again.

"But I have always been able to do that," she went on, "all my life, and I'm used to people's thoughts. I think you are a fine boy with a good mind. Before long you will be a good man and an able warrior. I tell you that honestly."

Nils grinned across at her.

"Our sword master curses me sometimes," Alvar launched on. "Quite often in fact. But he curses most of us a lot. He curses Ola least of all, and one of the Ukrainians the clan adopted that we have named Tryn because his nose is so big. They are the two best with swords in our whole ring.

"By the time the snow started to melt though, we were too hungry and didn't train much. And the horses were thin. Some of the old people died, and many of the Ukrainians. We left as soon as the ground was bare enough in the open and the horses could eat the dead grass. Ukrainian grass is very nourishing for horses. And as we traveled we ate everything we came across—deer, wild cattle, wild horses, wolves, hares—everything. The acorns bound up our bowels so that everyone was sick." He grimaced. "Then we made bark soup to loosen them, and that was worse. But since we arrived in the orc land we have had all the cattle we can eat, and fresh blood and milk to drink, so we are all hard-fleshed again and everyone feels strong.

"The People like this land. They didn't want to stay in the Ukraine because it was so poor in cattle, and the warriors say it is shameful to rob the Ukrainians who have so little." He shook his head. "But it's a pleasure to raid the orcish herds. And here we can live where the mountains meet the Great Meadow, with all the timber we need and endless pasture. We will force the orcs to attack us and then kill them. Kniv Listi is our war leader now. He is of the Weasel Clan, of the Jötar."

They were riding up a narrow foothill valley now, and Nils looked it over with interest. Its walls were forested, the south-facing with open pine stands, the opposite mostly with dense fir. The valley floor was meadow, encroached upon from the sides by pines and broken with groves of birch and aspen. A stream meandered about its midline, swollen by melting mountain snow.

Alvar chattered on. "Some of the mountain people attacked a party of us when we first camped here. They liked to hunt in this valley and wanted to drive us away. We let two of them go, and afterward a chief came who spoke some Anglic and talked with some of our people who speak it. The mountain folk are terrified of the orcs and do whatever they tell them, even deliver their prettiest girls. We told them we are going to kill all the orcs we can and drive the rest out of the country. We told them if they don't bother us we will not kill them, that it is only the orcs we feud with, but they must not spy on us for the orcs. A few of their young men have come to join us, and they are teaching us the country and some of the language."

Emerging from a birch grove they came in sight of a large encampment of tiny huts with low log walls, in loosely ordered rows instead of the customary neoviking ring. The clan totem stood near the center, a crude representation of an otter.

"We have not built real villages yet," Alvar explained. "It was decided we probably will have to move: we must be light on our feet. And the orcs will burn whatever we have built."

That night the Council of Chiefs and the War Council, from all the neoviking clans, met around a tall fire beneath the stars. A chieftain, referring to him as the Yngling, suggested that Nils Järnhann replace Kniv Listi as War Leader.

Nils stood in the circle of firelight, greasy braids resting on his wide heavy shoulders, and looked around him. "I thank Ulf Vargson for his faith in me. But I know of Kniv Listi, of his cunning and resourcefulness. His raids have been told of in the longhouse of my village. I prefer to leave the leadership in his experienced hands and act as counsel to him, as I did to Björn Ärrbuk when he led us in humiliating the orcs and horse barbarians time and again.

"Having said this, I will ask something of you. I would like to search the tribes for those who have prophetic dreams, or who sometimes seem to know what another will say before he says it. Some few of them will prove to have psi-power, as I have, but undeveloped. Trained, their minds can be as valuable to us as swords or bows."

VI

Tolkien conceived of Mordor,
stinking Mordor, wasteland, blasted,
land of vile depravities unnamed;
washed with reeking acid rain,
too corrupt for any greenness,
splintered mountains round a fissured plain.

For how could Mordor, foul, perverted,
smile beneath a sun?
How lie green with fragrant grass?
How lie spotted white and gold
with gently nodding flowers,
atrill with birdsong, sweet with loveliness?

From—EARTH, by Chandra Queiros

The *Phaeacia* resembled a giant guitar pick—a reflective ellipsoid seventy-one meters long, thirty-three wide, and somewhat thicker aft than foreward. Functional outriggings broke but did not spoil the symmetry of her lines. Much of her volume was occupied by the drive units, life support system, and a hangar for the two pinnaces. Living and working space for her crew of thirty-one and the sixteen members of the exploration team was adequate but tight.

A gong signalled three bells in the "afternoon" watch. The full exploration team and the ship's two ranking officers crowded into the narrow conference room to sit shoulder to shoulder around the polished hardwood table. When everyone was seated, Matthew Kumalo stood up. Conversation died and seventeen pairs of eyes settled on him.

"I've called us together to review the situation down below and how we'll approach it. If any of you think I'm wrong about it, I know I can trust you to tell me."

There were smiles around the table.

"Now I don't see us in any real danger down there if we're careful and use our heads. There is no possibility whatever that anyone on this planet has anything that can break our force shields. Any comments?"

"Yes." The speaker was Alex Malaluan, historian, who had studied everything available on research methods in archaeological anthropology. On New Home, of course, there was no such field, but the university library had material on it dating from old Earth. "Contact Prime stands on a part of the site of the old Romanian city of Constanta. So let's call it Constanta instead of Contact Prime. It sounds more like a place where people live—more human."

"Okay," said Matthew, "Constanta it is."

"What happened to the old city?" someone asked. "It hasn't been much more than seven hundred Earth years since it was a going concern."

"I expect the rounded hillocks we've seen, grown over with grass, are all that's left of it," Alex replied.

"How come? On some sites there are still some old buildings standing and a lot of recognizable rubble piles. Why are others like Constanta so smoothed over?"

Matthew interrupted. "Can you answer that in one hundred words or less, Alex? We need to get on with other things."

"Sure. Most towns and cities were built largely of materials not intended to last. They built buildings to knock down in twenty years or so, and replaced them with new ones that had newer engineering. They rejuvenated the material chemically and physically and remolded it for reuse. In some cities they made a point of maintaining selected old buildings or neighborhoods of stone or concrete construction, out of a sense of tradition; in fact a few old historical cities were quite largely maintained that way, although they were ringed with tracts of later, disposable-type construction. Those of us who flew over old Budapest were very impressed with the ruins there. But Constanta must have been virtually all late construction."

"And that's a subhumid climate they have there," Chandra put in. "Maybe even semiarid. Over the course of seven centuries they must have had some severe drought periods, some maybe lasting for decades. There would have been a lot of soil drifting over and around the rubble heaps in open country like that."

"Okay," Matthew cut in. "That was our hundred words. Now, the weapons chests aren't the place for the weapons any longer. Before we land we'll mount them where they'll be easy to get at if we need them."

"If we're going to have weapons handy," Chandra

said, "we'd better start with the clear understanding that they're a last resort. We came here to learn, not to intimidate anyone or make war."

"I think we're clear on that," Matthew replied mildly. "But if for some unforeseen reason we need weapons to keep from getting killed, then we'd better have them ready. Obviously though, our real security lies in being careful, using our heads, and keeping the force shields on except for leaving and entering the boats.

"Now a few last reminders. Don't land so close to any Earth person that he'll be inside your shield when you activate it. Unless of course you want him inside. And raise your commast before you activate. Otherwise you won't be able to hear or communicate with anyone outside without deactivating. And without the commast up it can get mighty stuffy inside the shield, fast.

"Also, at least to begin with I don't want both pinnaces to have people away from them at the same time without clearance. At least one has to be able to leave the ground at once, in case of emergency. The pinnaces, after all, are the only atmospheric flight capacity we have.

"And finally, everyone *will wear* a loaded pistol at all times when outside a shield, and carry two frag grenades with him, except in circumstances where it's clearly undesirable.

"Any questions or comments?"

"Yes."

The tone was heavy, dark, and all eyes went to Skipper Ram Uithoudt as he got to his feet. "Before we were treated to the discourse on archaeology, you said there was nothing whatever down there that could open our force shields. Well there is, and I'll bet there's a lot of it in everyday use."

The room was quiet for a moment before Matthew said, "What's that?"

"Trickery," Ram answered. "Trickery."

It was decided that *Alpha* would make first contact, with the same crew that had reconnoitered the city two days earlier. When she launched, she had a newly installed rack with automatic rifles ready for quick use. Two large open-topped bags hung beneath it, half full of fragmentation and blast grenades.

Draco rode with practiced ease. He'd spent thousands of hours in the saddle in his forty-four years, the first few hundred under the merciless eyes of hard-nosed drill instructors. Forty-four was rather old. Most died younger in battle or brawl, stabbings or beatings. To be not only forty-four but a consul was proof of outstanding ability and utter ruthlessness.

Right now he couldn't see the sky chariot; it was behind a hillock. When it had shown itself the other day, he'd been confident it would come to earth here sooner or later. He wondered if there were others.

He knew little about the ancients, but the old stories told of great power. They could smash a city flat with no more effort than a man squashing a bug beneath his foot. The only reasons they could have for returning were to rule or collect tribute. They might want a regent to administer for them here, or a go-between, someone who knew situations and possibilities.

He turned to scowl at Ahmed's small group par-
alleling his own a dozen meters away. It was a
nuisance to have to screen out here on the steppe.
To preserve his privacy and vanity, Draco had no
psi on his immediate staff, relying entirely on his
own powerful talent. But the non-psi Sudanese
dog kept two of them with him everywhere but in
harem, including that insolent eunuch, Yusuf the
Turk.

Topping the low rise, he could see the sky chariot atop the next gentle hillock, shining brightly in
the sun. Did they use slaves to polish it, he
wondered, or did their arts keep it so? The last few
score meters they rode warily, observing with care.
A few meters from the sky chariot was a curved
line of crushed grass and broken flowers, as if, for
some reason, people within it had come out and
trampled an exactly circular path around their
craft.

The two groups of horsemen had almost come
together now, converging on the pinnace. Ahmed
was a length ahead when Draco, about to spur
even, saw Ahmed's stallion recoil, its powerful
haunches bunched, and try to back away as if it
had bumped into something. Draco reined to an
abrupt stop and watched while Ahmed brought
his now-rearing mount under control, using the
spade-bit brutally.

Tentatively Draco moved his horse toward the
pinnace with short steps. At the line in the grass it
jerked its head and nearly squatted as it took a
reflexive step backward. Then both men turned
their nervous animals and sidled toward the craft,
each with one hand outstretched. Something hard

was there that they could not see, something un-
yielding that rose from the ring of flattened grass.

At that moment the sky chariot turned to glass
before them, and Draco could see the people
inside—five of them. Strange clothing covered
them from foot to neck, fitting their limbs loosely.
Surrounded by an invisible wall, they wore no
body armor. And no swords; perhaps the small
objects belted to their waists were weapons of
some kind.

They were looking at him and his people.

Probably the invisible wall would allow weapons to be wielded outwardly by those inside, even
though it apparently would let nothing penetrate
from without.

But it did not block thoughts effectively. And
they thought in Anglic; that was a stroke of luck!
The Master had made his officers learn the language because it was widely used in Europe between people of different native tongues.

Abruptly a voice spoke, loud and clear, seeming
somehow to come from a spar extending above the
chariot. The tone was slightly metallic but clearly
a woman's. Her aura was not one you would find
about a slave; among the ancients, as among some
peoples on Earth, women must rank as men.

The audio pickup in the commast seemed to be
working well, Matthew noted. It was directional,
and right now was focused on two who appeared
to be the leaders and who sat their horses side by
side. Their breast plates were burnished silver instead of bronze, and their helmets more luxuri-
antly plumed. The shorter of the two replied to
Nikko's question.

"Yes, we speak Anglic, but it is not our native speech."

"What is your native speech?" Nikko asked.

His answer meant nothing to her, but Anne Marie said softly, "Let me have the mike." She spoke into it in an unfamiliar language, listened, then turned to the others. "Arabic," she said, "or rather, a twenty-ninth century derivative. It's not much like the computer extrapolations of what Arabic might have become. More like a pidgin Arabic, as if . . ."

"What did he say?" Matthew interrupted with some irritation.

"It amounted to flattery and a formal welcome. They are honored to talk to the ancients, and something about helping us in any way they can. That's the gist of it."

Their scabbards were conspicuously empty. *They're bound to be impressed with the pinnace,* Matthew told himself, *and they probably have legends of laser weapons, nuclear bombs, the whole ancient armory, though God knows what transformations they may have undergone over centuries of oral tradition. It's just as well they don't know we don't have such things today.*

Mikhail voiced similar thoughts. "Eating out of our hands, sounds like. I wouldn't let them know how little we have in the way of ordnance and men; they might turn less respectful."

Matthew nodded. "Anne, tell them we've come from a world of the ancients, in a great starship that's hovering five hundred kilometers directly above their city. They may not know what a kilometer is, so explain to them that the ship is above the sky, where there is no air to breathe and it's always night. That should impress them."

"I'm not up to that on short notice, Chief. I'll need some review before I get very ambitious."

"Use Anglic then. It should help strengthen our psychological dominance if they have to use our language. Tell them we don't want to harm them. Say we want to know more about them and . . . no, wait. We'd better sound more business-like. Ask who their ruler is."

As Anne Marie spoke, Matthew watched the two leaders. They consulted briefly in whispers too soft for the pickup to adjust to, but he got the impression that they were not friendly to one another.

The one who answered was not the one who had spoken before. "I am Ahmed and he is Draco. We rule together since the death of our great Master, Kazi, who was already great among the ancients, your forefathers. He fathered our people and ruled them from their beginning."

"Wow!" Anne Marie exclaimed when he was done. "Sounds like they have some fantastic traditions. I can hardly wait to find out about them."

"And they rule together," Matthew mused. "Somehow I don't believe that's a happy and stable arrangement. Ask them the name of their nation."

The shorter man answered again, back straight, head high. "Our nation is the Empire of Kazi. That is the City of Kazi and we are the Orcs."

"Orcs," Nikko said to herself, and frowned thoughtfully. Somewhere, she was sure, she had read or heard of orcs. Her mind sought back through courses in history, Earth geography, anthropology, but nothing came to her. Whatever orcs had been though, the word stirred aversion and distrust within her.

"Tell them we want to know more about them," Matthew was saying. "Tell them we're going to send two ambassadors among them. Tell them . . . tell them they are to treat our ambassadors as royalty and to answer all questions honestly and completely, or we will be angry with them. Got that?"

Anne Marie repeated it before switching the microphone on. Matthew searched the unreadable expressions of the listening orcs while she broadcast.

"I never knew you were so tough," Mikhail murmured with a grin.

"Power is something these people obviously understand and appreciate," Matthew answered. "If they think we have a lot of it, we'll hold their respect. And as far as that's concerned, can you imagine what we could do to them with our grenades and automatic weapons from an aircraft?"

Mikhail grunted. "The threat's the thing though. Tough-looking characters like that would never imagine we wouldn't follow through."

The orc leaders consulted in whispers for minutes before answering; finally the one called Ahmed faced the *Alpha* again. "It will be necessary to prepare a proper apartment for our royal guests. We will be ready to receive ambassadors tomorrow."

"Tell them we'll be here at midday," Matthew instructed, "with two ambassadors, a man and a woman. We'll expect them to be furnished everything they wish in the way of comforts and servants. Tell them we are used to the best, and will expect the best when we are among them."

Abruptly when Anne Marie finished, Matthew deactivated the shield and lifted *Alpha* vertically with sudden speed, out of sight without farewell.

Nikko raised her eyebrows at her husband. "You're not exactly a paragon of courtesy today."

He didn't smile. "We'll let the ambassadors be the diplomats. I want them to think of me as hard and mean."

"Who are your ambassadors going to be?" Chandra asked expectantly. "They ought to include someone who speaks the language, don't you think? And her husband?"

Matthew glanced over his shoulder at Chandra's grin, and his unaccustomed grimness passed. "I tried to fix it so you wouldn't even have to pack. Assuming Anne is willing."

Anne's voice and face were sober. "Of course. This is the kind of thing we came all this way for."

"Like royalty," Chandra said, rubbing his hands together. "I think we're about to learn what the term 'Roman splendor' means."

Draco glanced sourly toward Ahmed nearby, into whose ears Yusuf was pouring all they'd gleaned from the thoughts of the star men. Amazing that the ancients exposed their thoughts so freely. It was obvious they had no awareness at all of telepathy.

They rode on toward the City, both Draco and Ahmed digesting what they had learned, their earlier awe of the ancients replaced by a compound of greed and caution. Now they would have to agree on where, in the palace, the ambassadors would be quartered. It might take an adjustment of sectors to find a suitable apartment in a neutral location; neither would willingly let the other have control of them.

Nikko Kumalo's searching had reached a dead end. She could not place the word *orc.*

In their small cabin aboard the *Phaeacia* she listened to Matthew's slow even breathing. Usually she fell asleep quickly, but tonight her riddle had kept her awake. She had asked the computer what the word meant. It had printed out—ORC: ANY OF SEVERAL LARGE FISH-LIKE MAMMALS OF EARTH, ESPECIALLY *GRAMPUS GRISEUS.*

But her subconscious insisted that was not the source of the word's familiarity.

It would come to her eventually, she was sure.

VII

Within the City of Kazi were approximately 22,000 slaves.[127]

In a totally despotic society it can be difficult to define "slave"; in a sense, everyone below the ruling class is a slave. Within the context of the orc society, I have classified as slaves all who were not orcs.

A majority of the slaves, roughly 18,000 of them, were women and girls who served several purposes. They did most of the common labor and almost all of the domestic service. They provided the major sexual outlet for the orcs and were the source of almost all the vicious boy children who grew up, or more often died, in the rigid and brutalizing orcling pens. The orcs were the children of the slaves, and it was the orcs who victimized the slaves.[128]

Slaves also provided the skilled labor and professional services upon which the city depended. They were the stone masons, smiths, armor artificers, mechanics; the civil engineers, physicians, accountants and bureaucrats. Skilled slaves enjoyed a degree of protection from the capricious cruelty and casual abuse of the soldiers, the degree of protection depending on the importance of the slave and the rank of the soldier. Slaves who were important enough were allowed to have families—in a very few cases even small harems or androecia—and given apartments. The consul Ahmed was the son of one such slave, although to apply the term "slave" in such a case rather stretches the concept.

But except at the uppermost level, security was tenuous even for the slave elite. An imprudent thought monitored by an orc telepath, an unintended offense to an officer, a momentary lapse in one's servility, could collapse that small "private" world and expose the slave to the full force of orc brutality.[129]

In such a society one might expect an underground to exist. But in a society using telepathic surveillance and ruthless repression—given to uninhibited and in fact mandatory sadism—that underground was certain to be small, fearful, and largely ineffectual.

Over the years there must have been innumerable small acts of opportunistic sabotage carried out on the spur of the moment by individuals and involving no conspiracy.[130] But the term "underground" does not include such unaffiliated individuals. The real underground, in the sense of conspiratorial groups, consisted primarily of artisans and bureaucrats, slaves with some degree of private life—a slave intelligentsia, so to speak. It also included a very few orcs who had been sensitized by attachment to some slave and who had reacted against the culture which ravaged the slave.[131]

Apparently the underground groups were all very small and not generally in contact with one another.

A substantial part of their small total membership seems to have consisted of telepaths. In the underground, telepaths would seem to have a better chance of surviving than non-telepaths. And perhaps telepaths tend to have more empathy for other humans, although Kazi, a remarkably able telepath, was nothing less than satanic.

Interestingly, one of the principal members of the underground was one of Kazi's daughters, Nephthys. Nephthys was also the prized and privileged jewel in the harem of Draco, one of the two ruling consuls after Kazi's death.

From—A HISTORY OF THE ORCS, by Reinholdt
    Malaluan. A.C. 876, Deep Harbor,
    New Home

VIII

Orc officers were skilled in subterfuge and concealment of purpose. They practiced them unceasingly
in the vicious politics of command. But in those
politics, *character* concealment was neither troubled with nor possible; they were too much alike,
and too many were telepaths.

Now, when it might have been possible to conceal
their character from their visitors, they didn't
know how. Both assigned hosts wore togas instead
of uniforms, but their arrogance, hardness, and
utter lack of compassion were increasingly apparent
with continued contact.

In contrast, Chandra and Anne Marie were conspicuously innocent, earnest, and benign.

The driver, standing against the dashboard of
the polished and topless bronze chariot, was like
none of his passengers. He was a non-personality
whom his masters would notice only in failure or
error, unless one of them was looking for someone
to abuse. To Chandra and Anne Marie, he was
silently informative, a source of inner discomfort.

Their first afternoon had been spent with their
two hosts beneath an awning on one of the roof

gardens of the varied-level palace. What had been anticipated as a session of questions and answers had proved to be a round of frustration. It became clear that their hosts would not be frank, and they in turn dared not be. But the orc telepaths had learned abundantly from their unspoken thoughts and reactions.

At Chandra's request, much of the subsequent two days had been spent seeing the city, and their cameras had been busy. Yesterday they had visited the squat cylindrical granaries and seen how barges would be unloaded in harvest time. Blindfolded oxen trod in circles, turning a heavy capstan that powered a conveyor screw. The cats that policed the granaries seemed as arrogant and efficient as the orcs.

Today's visit had been to a slaughterhouse where women cut up carcasses of beef, their strong bare arms smeared with blood. The floors were mortared stone, sloping to drains and scrubbed daily with lye. From the slaughterhouse the ambassadors had been taken upstream to the water intake plant, where the long vanes of windmills pumped canal water into tanks resembling the granaries. The stout bald man in charge had bowed and smiled and rubbed his hands. A man of responsibility, he none the less wore numerals tattooed on his forehead, like their driver and the women in the slaughterhouse and every other unarmed inhabitant they'd noticed.

Afterward Anne Marie had ridden in preoccupied silence. Now she looked around again. *From the air I thought this place was handsome*, she told herself, *but it's not. It's ugly*. Nothing green, noth-

ing growing except on and around the palace. Just
stone buildings and hectares on hectares of pavement. At least they'd had the foresight to install
lots of storm drains. But why no soil, no grass, no
trees? Two-storied row buildings of precisely fitted stone blocks crowded the wide streets. Their
windows were small in the thick walls, giving
built-in tunnel vision.

From the air they had seen substantial grounds
separating the buildings from those behind them.
She thought she knew now what they were: drill
grounds. She couldn't remember whether they had
looked paved or not, and tried to glimpse them
through the alleyways between buildings. But the
alleyways were long and narrow; from the moving
chariot her eyes were rewarded by nothing more
than momentary slots of light.

The hard-faced officers sat facing them; she and
Chandra thought of them as "the Centurions." What
were they thinking, sitting so expressionlessly?

Chandra broke the silence. "Why have most of
the workers we've seen been women?"

"The men have been taken into the army," one
of the officers recited. "Barbarians threaten the
country, and we must defend it."

"From the sky we saw a fight between barbarians and some of your cavalry. Then we flew over
their encampment. There aren't enough of them to
endanger the Empire of Kazi or this city."

Neither "centurion" spoke for perhaps a minute.
Finally the second one replied. "Many thousands
more are scattered through the country northwest
of the sea. They have laid waste the country there,
butchering the inhabitants and burning the towns."

"Where do you keep the children?" Anne Marie asked. "All I've seen are girls at least ten years old. I haven't seen any boys at all. Where do you keep them?"

The two faces turned to her, and somehow made that simple act a communication of contempt. "Children are kept separate so that the women may work without hindrance. They live in separate quarters."

"But who brings them up? Who takes care of them?"

"Those who are assigned."

She persisted. "When can we visit them?"

"I do not know."

They were grateful to reach the palace grounds, to be led by a steward to their luxurious quarters.

The upper levels of the palace consisted of numerous segments of terraces, some of them entirely gardens, others with one or more apartments opening onto gardens. Chandra and Anne Marie had a terrace, with its apartment, to themselves. After supper they found their reclining chairs had been moved into the shade of three neatly sheared cedars where they could sit out of the evening sun. A small olive-colored bird sang energetically in a low waxy-leaved tree.

Anne Marie gestured at the chairs. "Moved again. I'm afraid our privacy is fictitious."

"The price of service, I suppose. At least they're quiet and inconspicuous."

"And efficient."

"The whole outfit is efficient." With a grunt Chandra lowered himself into one of the chairs. "I don't know why I ate so much, unless it was to make up for a lousy day."

"I suppose frustration is part of being an ambassador," she replied. "And it hasn't been a total loss. We're getting a pretty good idea of their technology and the kind of people they are. And a lot of good video footage."

She walked to the balustrade and looked northward across the city's roofs. "What kind of games do you suppose they play in that big stadium?"

"The word is *arena.* A stadium implies athletic contests. I'd be surprised if they didn't set tigers loose on the slaves over there. I've got the feeling they'd feed them babies without blinking."

"Do you suppose they're going to let us see the children?" she asked.

"I doubt it. The boy children are probably in barracks somewhere, getting military training. I think the women are slaves and most of the men are soldiers. Mike was right: This city has no walls because it has a big tough professional army. And who but slaves would wear numbers tattooed on their foreheads?"

They both remained silent for awhile.

"Maybe we shouldn't be so critical of the orcs," Anne Marie said thoughtfully. "They have to cope with a pretty hard and warlike world. Like those barbarians."

"Don't blame the barbarians for the orcs; not that pack of barbarians anyway. The orcs said they're just arriving, but this city and its culture have been around for awhile."

He got to his feet. "I think it's time to call Matt again, and this time I won't mince words."

*   *   *

On the *Phaeacia,* Matthew looked unseeingly at the instrument panel for a long moment after Chandra broke transmission.

"Huh! Whatever those people are, they've made a rotten impression on Chan and Anne. What do you make of it?"

"Well," Nikko answered, "when he said that about 'feeding them babies,' I remembered what orcs were. Orcs in ancient literature, that is."

"Oh? What?"

"An army of subhuman monsters."

Matthew looked at her, perplexed.

"It was in a fantasy I read when I was about fourteen or fifteen—a trilogy, THE LORD OF THE RINGS. In the story there was an evil sorcerer, a super sorcerer, who'd lived for centuries. Millennia, in fact. And he'd bred an army of sadistic subhuman monsters called orcs, and tried to conquer the world with them. He even had a black tower, like the city down there."

"Isn't that a little—improbable? Ancient literature—fantasy literature, anyway—is unlikely to have survived down there. They *must* have gotten the word from something else. Don't you think?"

Nikko shrugged. "All the computer had to say about 'orc' was, a fish-like marine mammal of Earth. And there are an awful lot of parallels between what's down there and what's in the book. What I'm concerned about is the kind of society it would be that tried to emulate the land of Mordor."

Matthew leaned back and pulled briefly on his chin. "I think I'll call a team meeting for oh-eight hundred tomorrow," he said reflectively. "Maybe we need a different contact, for a little perspective."

"A different contact? With whom?"

"How about some simple straightforward savages this time? The barbarians. It ought to be interesting and even informative. And there shouldn't be any danger in it. We can just sit in the pinnace with the force shield on and talk to them from there."

IX

Sågs d' förste a en pojke
dä d' svävte uppi himlen
jussom örn ör lunna vannen
när d' stirra ned på jedden
simne upp t' jämna ytan.
Röpte höd å pekte uppe.
"Dä jussom kjämpnar tälte om,
som döjtsa häxen sejte
bärar gamlarna fra sjäänor."

[It was first a child that saw it,
saw it hovering in the morning
like an eagle over water
watching ready for the salmon
rising to the quiet surface.
Called aloud and pointed upward.
" 'tis the thing the warriors spoke of,
that the German seeress told us
carries ancients from the stars."]

From—THE JÄRNHANN SAGA,
Kumalo translation

It settled slowly like a polished silver bowl, oblong, inverted, and with stubby legs, while children of all sizes ran toward it through the meadow, looking upward. The audio pickup brought calling voices and the barking of a few dogs. Three meters from the ground, Matthew had to stop descent; there wasn't enough room to set down and activate the shield without trapping children inside.

"How about that!" Mikhail said. "They're not a bit afraid. You'd think space craft landed here every week and passed out candy."

Matthew picked up the microphone and, with the volume turned high, ordered them to clear room for landing. The only effect was to increase the volume of shrill voices.

A number of men and women were approaching now on foot and horseback, most of them moving casually, neither hurrying nor hanging back. As they reached the vicinity they formed small groups behind the children, watching with apparent interest and talking easily among themselves.

"Should I transvise?" Mikhail asked.

"Sure, go ahead," said Matthew, and the hubbub swelled as the mob of children could suddenly see through the hull.

More adults and children were arriving. A very large man on horseback picked his way through the children, who opened a path for him. When he reached the center he raised both arms overhead and the tumult subsided a bit.

"T'baka Du!" he called. "Gö klar för skybåten!"

"I understood that!" Nikko said excitedly. "He told them to move back and give us room. It's something like Swedish; I'll bet I can talk to them!"

The children were backing away, with some of

the older boys taking charge, giving orders and gesturing. When the loose throng had become a circle, Matthew put the *Alpha* down and instantly activated the shield. Then they sat without speaking, watching the children discover the shield and test it with curious hands.

"All right," Matthew said at last. "Try your Swedish on them and see how it goes. Say we wish them no harm and do not like to use our great weapons which can kill large numbers from a distance."

Nikko pressed the microphone switch and an "Ah-h-h" ran through the crowd as she began speaking slowly in a tonal cadence. When she had finished, the man who'd moved the children signalled the crowd to quiet once more. He hadn't taken time to saddle his mount, but sat it bareback, sideways now. His left foot dangled; his right leg was cocked up on the animal's back. It would have been hard to look more nonchalant.

"We are pleased you speak our language," he said, speaking it himself for the crowd. "It is very rare to find a foreigner who does. But it will be better if I talk in Anglic; then we need not wait while the woman translates for you. I will tell my people afterward what was said. They are glad you have come. We want to be friends with the star people."

There was a murmur of assent from the crowd while Nikko translated.

"Ask him how he knows we are star people," Matthew instructed. Nikko spoke, still in Swedish, and many of the children looked back toward the nearby huts, pointing and calling out.

"I'm not getting all that," Nikko told the others.

"Something about a witch, apparently, a döjtsa witch, whatever that is."

Again the big man spoke, in Anglic this time. "Who but the star people would come out of the sky? Besides, my wife foretold your coming; it is she the children called a witch. And also, your force shield does not stop thoughts."

"Let me have the microphone," Matthew said. Nikko handed it to him and he thumbed the switch. "What do you know about force shields?" he demanded.

"Only the little your thoughts have told me, and what I observe in the children."

"Damn it, Matt!" Mikhail said. "Don't you see what he's saying? The man's a telepath! He even knew that Nikko is the only one of us that speaks Swedish!"

Matthew digested that for a few seconds, then set it aside for the time. "Who is your ruler?" he asked. "We want to talk to him."

"The Council of Chiefs has been sent for and should be here after a while. But I am the only one of them who speaks Anglic. My name is Nils Järnhann."

The man sat his horse no more than six meters away, just outside the shield, and Matthew looked him over carefully. He'd stand at least 195 centimeters and mass 110 kilos. Even relaxed he gave an impression of great strength and virility, like a jungle cat. He wore soft leather breeches wrapped around his calves with strips. Short blond braids reached his burly shoulders. The thinness of his mustache and beard suggested youth, despite his physique and presence and apparent rank.

"How did you come to learn Anglic when your people don't speak it?" Matthew asked.

"When we still lived in the north I was cast out for a killing, and wandered in countries where Anglic was spoken between those of different tongues."

"How did you live in exile?"

"As a soldier and assassin."

"And why did your people take you back again?"

"When they left our homeland they had need of an Yngling."

Matthew turned to Nikko. "What's an Ingling?"

She shrugged. "It used to mean a youth, a youngling, but that doesn't fit the context here. It must have picked up a different meaning along the line, or a special connotation."

Matthew switched on the microphone again. "What brings your people to this land which is claimed by the orcs?"

"Our homeland grows colder and wetter year by year. It was harder and harder to make a crop. The turnips rotted in the field and the rye molded in the shocks. People of middle age remember when cattle could graze for five or six months of the year. In recent years it was necessary to feed hay for eight months, while the hay crops grew poorer. In the north among the reindeer and glutton clans, things were even worse. Finally, a year ago, the ground was still snow-covered in June. The tribes made peace, united, and left—left a land that had been their mother but could no longer feed them."

A land they knew and loved, thought Matthew. No doubt the only land most of them had been able to imagine. That must have been a hard decision.

"The People crossed the sea in boats," the man continued. "We allied ourselves with the Poles and others and defeated the armies of Kazi that had come to conquer Europe. After a winter of hunger, the People came to this place. We like it here. It is rich in grass and cattle. There is timber for fuel and building. We will stay and drive the orcs away."

"Are these your entire people, camped along this valley?"

"Yes."

"There are many more orcs than there are of you. What makes you think you can drive them out?"

"The orcs are strong and dangerous, but not as strong as you think. They are like a great spruce tree, mighty, darkening much ground and shading out what takes root beneath them, but rotten and hollow inside. For outlanders they are skilled fighters, but now that Kazi is dead, there is nothing they live for and nothing they are willing to die for. They have pride, but even that is shallow. They obey because they hardly know how to disobey and they are afraid to disobey, but they find no savor in risking life, only in taking it."

"How do you know so much about the orcs?"

"I have been in their city, been their prisoner, talked with Kazi himself and fought in their arena. Their language is strange to me, but I could see their pictures and look through their eyes and know their feelings. And of course, we have met them in war."

Matthew changed direction. "And you were an assassin? How many men did you kill?"

"As an assassin, none. I was sent by the Inner

Circle of the Kinfolk, the Psi Alliance, to assassinate Kazi, but I failed. It was in war I killed him."

Inner Circle. Psi Alliance. I'm glad we're getting this on tape, Matthew thought.

The big Northman sat quietly for a moment, and Matthew felt the man's gaze. Then Nils Järnhann spoke again. "I have answered your questions. Now I will tell you things you have more need to know. You have left friends, people you love, a man and a woman, with the orcs. They are not safe. The orcs find their pleasure in giving pain, in breaking the body and mind. Especially tender minds. Your friends, if they are like you, must be very tempting to them."

Until then Matthew had affected a faint hauteur; it was replaced now by wary intentness. The Northman continued, his voice seeming to grow louder, driving the words into their minds like a hammer.

"And how could that happen to the Star People? But you are few, and your weapons are not so powerful as you pretend. And you are not hard-minded: killing, violence, are foreign and unnatural to you, difficult to do or even to think about.

"And the orcs know that. They have many telepaths. They know every thought your friends have had since they have been among them, every word they have said in privacy. They have heard with their ears and seen with their eyes and felt their feelings. *And they have shared their rememberings.*"

A coldness washed through Matthew, a desolate sense of naked helplessness, a nightmare feeling of isolation hundreds of light years from the safe space of home. He was gripped by an urgent need to escape the Northman's words and the mind that looked so relentlessly into theirs.

"Let's get out of here," he said to the others. "We need to think and talk." Looking through the hull at Nils Järnhann, he thumbed the microphone switch again. "We'll be back in an hour—before the sun is much higher." With that he deactivated and sent *Alpha* sharply upward, not stopping until they were above the troposphere. He parked on the encampment vector, eighteen kilometers above the surface, and for a long moment no one spoke.

"Does anyone here have anything to say?" Matthew asked.

"Maybe we'd better get Chan and Anne out of that city," Mikhail suggested, "while they're still ambassadors instead of hostages. It would be damned attractive to the orcs to trade them for a pinnace complete with automatic rifles and grenades. And consider what that would mean in ruthless hands like theirs!"

Carlos Lao was a biologist who didn't often say much. He spoke now. "We don't actually know that the barbarian was telling the truth."

"He must have been," Nikko replied. "It fits with what Chan and Anne told us about the orcs, and with the implications of their calling themselves orcs in the first place."

"You misunderstand me," Carlos told her. "What I meant was, we don't really know the orcs have telepaths."

"I'm accepting it as a working assumption," Matthew said. "There's no doubt the barbarian's a telepath, so why not some orcs too? Now, accepting that the orcs have telepaths monitoring them, how do we get them out? We can't let Chan or

Anne know what we're doing. Otherwise the orcs will know too."

They discussed the matter a little longer. "Okay," Matthew said, "I think we know what we have to do. Now, in a few minutes we'll be on the ground again, talking to the barbarian. We're going to follow up this contact; as short as it was, it's already been extremely valuable. But I don't want to commit anyone else as an ambassador. What would you think of inviting them to send someone with us to the *Phaeacia*?"

"As long as he leaves his sword at home," Mikhail said. "And his scalping knife."

This time the meadow held hundreds of adults, both men and women. The children formed a loose ring outside them now, partly watching and partly chasing and tussling like two-legged puppies. In the middle of the throng an opening had been left perhaps twenty meters across, and Matthew landed there. A group of men, mostly middle-aged or older, moved in to form a semi-circle just outside the shield. Nikko assumed they were the Council of Chiefs. Three of them, presumably the principal chiefs, were uniquely dressed and stood together. One was a very tall old man wearing a long cloak of white bird skins, with the skin of a white wolf's head as a headdress. His beard completed the theme of white. A second was nearly as tall, with a short cape of heavy white fur and a headpiece Nikko tentatively identified as from an arctic bear. He was missing a hand, but his exposed legs still were strongly muscled, his red beard only streaked with gray. The third too favored white, a short cape of white fur spotted with black, which Nikko recognized from old pictures as ermine. Instead of head fur, he wore a steel helmet onto which great curved steel horns had been fitted. He was shorter than the other two but still taller than average, his body thick with the muscles of a man of fifty who continues a hard and strenuous life.

Nils Järnhann stood next to the tallest of the three, and about as tall. Järnhann. The name was easy for Nikko to remember because she knew its meaning—Ironhand. He spoke a few quiet words to the man in the feathered cloak. The old chief answered quietly, then turned his proud face to *Alpha* and spoke slowly and distinctly in Scandinavian.

"We are the Council of Chiefs. Nils Järnhann tells us one of you speaks our language, though not well. We hope you will speak it now so that all of us understand."

Nikko held the microphone, phrasing as well as she could in twenty-first-century Swedish what the four of them had agreed upon before coming back down.

"We want to be friends with your people, and with all the people of Earth. This was the world of our forefathers. We come to you from a world called New Home, whose thousands of thousands of people sent us to see what had become of this world, which we call Earth."

The old man's sober expression had not changed. "We are pleased that you have come among us, the *People*. You chose well. We are not numerous, but we are first in honor and cunning and weapon skills."

When Nikko had finished interpreting, Carlos grunted. "Every culture is honorable in its own eyes. What brand of honor goes with pride in cunning, I wonder?"

Nikko spoke again to the Northmen: "We wish to know all the people of Earth, to learn what they believe, what they honor, and how they live. We hope that one of you will come among us for a short while to tell us about yourselves and also to learn about us."

"You should stay among us, instead," the old man answered. "That is the way to learn how we live and act, observing as well as asking questions."

"Perhaps we will, later on."

The man with the horned helmet spoke this time, his tone surly and his words too quick for Nikko to follow until he repeated them. "How do we know you would treat that person honorably and send him back? You are not of the People. You are foreigners. We do not know whether you are honorable."

"At least one of you can read our minds," Nikko answered, "the one named Nils Järnhann. Let him say whether we are honorable."

The chiefs looked at Nils, waiting for him to speak. A woman had stepped beside him, big with child, and he put an arm around her. "My wife says she would willingly go with you. But while I sense no treachery in you, who knows what may happen tomorrow that might take you away from our world, and her with you? I would not let her go unless one of you stays with us—the woman Nikko, who speaks our language."

Matthew stared at him as Nikko finished translating. *The bastard*! Cunning, they'd said. What was the man up to? Nikko's hand was on his arm, and he looked at her. She wanted to go; her earnest eyes left no doubt. "I can't let you," he said "It could be dangerous."

"She's willing to put herself in our hands, and he's willing to let her. On this world we'll never have better insurance than that."

Matthew groped mentally for a reason to refuse "If you stayed here, who on *Phaeacia* could talk to her?"

From the audio pickup a woman's voice interrupted them in Anglic. "I volunteered because I would like to learn from you also. And I speak your language. I must tell you first, however, that I did not grow up among the Northmen. I am German."

Matthew eyed her carefully. Big-boned, young and very very pregnant. The man was risking his wife and his child too.

"But I have come to know these people well," she continued, "and understand them, because I am a telepath. I can also tell you about my homeland and its people, and about the Psi Alliance, for I am of the Kinfolk. It is the Kinfolk who have kept alive the stories of the past."

"Careful, Matt," Carlos warned softly. "She's a telepath. Why should she push the exchange like that unless they're up to something? She may not even be his wife!"

Nikko turned sharply to the biologist. "Don't get paranoid on us, Carl! Remember, Ram's a telepath too, if only now and then! And as for pushing it—she wants to know, to learn. That's what *we're* supposed to be doing; that's what this expedition is all about!" She looked back to Matthew. "Remember what the chidren called his wife before? The Döjtsa Häxen—the German witch! Only I didn't recognize their word for German because instead of the old Swedish word, *tyska*, they used an approximation of the German word, *deutsche*. Matt, she'll be a treasure chest of information!"

Matthew looked around at the others. "She's right; it's what we came here for. It's a rare opportunity, and she'll be as much security for Nikko as Nikko is for her."

At least I hope so, he added somberly to himself.

X

Stor tidragen han t' flikkor,
ofta kjikt i ham på sölstig
blikkor fölte ham på midda,
nog dröd när en mö i sjymning,
viskte bjääli t' vä ellen.

[Fascinating he to women,
often glanced at him by morning,
followed him their eyes at midday,
lingered near sometimes at twilight,
whispered to him in the firelight.]

From—THE JÄRNHANN SAGA,
Kumalo translation

Each low hovel of small unsquared logs had two doors through which one passed crouching, and sod roofs with a central smoke hole. Inside they reeked of wood smoke.

Women moved about the camp carrying wood or water or simply going somewhere, often accompanied by small children or older girls. Other children followed Nils and Nikko, and she tested her

Swedish on them, turning to Nils for help when she failed to understand or be understood. Already she was beginning to see patterns in the language changes; as she learned them she'd communicate more effectively.

Her pocket video camera was often in her hands.

She looked up at Nils. "Why did you make a temporary camp if you expect to drive the orcs out of the country?"

"Because the orcs will probably come and destroy it. It wouldn't be realistic to defend it. And when they leave the country we'll spread out by clans, perhaps one clan to a valley. We're too many to live so close very long, but for now we stay together so we can gather forces quickly when we want to. Would you like to see some of our men training?"

She said she would, and they left the proximity of the huts for an open grassy field where sweating boys and men with wooden swords and leather shields thrust and parried. They ranged from early adolescence to middle age. Drill masters moved among them, stopping individuals, talking to them, demonstrating, occasionally berating. Nearby were irregular groups of little boys with sticks and small shields, frequently watching, often sparring or shadow-sparring, and sometimes racing or wrestling. She realized now why these people were so strong.

"Why are some of the instructors younger than so many of the men they're training?" Nikko asked.

"The instructors are warriors, some as young as nineteen. The older men in training are freeholders—farmers not trained before to fight. Warriors learn their skills from boyhood by training long days, until every act, every move and response, comes quickly and correctly without thought. These farmers will never equal warriors, but they are strong and proud, and the best will be as good as most orcs. Until they are thirteen or fourteen, most of them spent a lot of time practicing with sticks, like those little fellows out there, earning lots of sore spots. And as bowmen they're already very good. All their lives they've shot at marks, and hunted game to help feed themselves and their families.

"In the past the bans protected them from war, but the bans mean nothing to orcs. And while the warriors will protect them as much as they can, the freeholders must be ready to protect themselves if they need to."

"Freeholders," Nikko said. "Do you have slaves then?"

"We used to—warriors taken prisoner from other clans in raids. But after we united, the thralls returned to their own clans. Now all men are freeholders."

"Don't you mean all men are either freeholders or warriors?"

"In a sense. Warriors are freeholders too, but a warrior is special. In the homeland he worked his own land, but had the help of slaves to give him time to practice with weapons."

"And I suppose warriors consider themselves better than other freeholders."

Nils nodded. "To be chosen by the clan as a sword apprentice, to become a warrior, was a great honor. And a warrior is proud of being a warrior. But a warrior's father often is simply a farmer, yet the son honors him. Also, a warrior's sons often will not be chosen, will simply be farmers, yet they are his sons and he will love and respect them. And a warrior will have been simply a farmer in past lives, and perhaps a slave in one to come."

That startled Nikko Kumalo. "Do your people believe in rebirth then?"

"Of course."

"And do you remember, uh, past lives?"

"No. To die is to forget. Sometimes a little child remembers, and occasionally an old person, but it is usually a little glimpse, unclear and often uncertain."

So, she thought, they may not be afraid to die. "How do you decide who will be a warrior?"

"In their thirteenth or fourteenth summer, boys were selected for size and strength, and skill in war-play, to become sword apprentices. In their nineteenth summer they became warriors. But that is changing now."

"Why haven't your people killed each other off over the years?"

"The bans set limits and rules for fighting between clans and tribes. Few but warriors were killed."

"But then, warriors must be more likely to die young. If you select the strongest and quickest to become warriors, in the course of time your people will become weaker."

He shook his head, smiling. "Warriors can have several wives, other men but one. And it isn't unusual for women to seek the attention of a warrior. Among our women, warriors are considered desirable lovers."

"And what do their husbands do if they find out?"

"Beat them."

"Beat the wife, you mean?"

"Yes."

"But why the wife?"

"The wife has insulted him by turning to another man, so he beats her."

"And nothing is done to the warrior?"

"No. He has honored the woman's husband by finding his wife desirable."

"But . . ." Nikko started to protest, then realized the futility of it and asked instead, "What if an unmarried girl gets pregnant by a warrior?"

"Unless the warrior marries her, the child is taken from her and grows up in the warrior's family as his child. Then, because she was desirable to a warrior, other men will want to marry her."

"How many wives do you have, Nils?"

"One."

"Only one?"

"There may be others later. Ilse will remain the principal wife."

They had left the training field, wandering along the river to a high cutbank where children were swimming.

"The orcs looked very tough and disciplined, and there are a lot of them. Do you really expect to beat them?"

Nils nodded. "We beat them badly in every fight. Partly it was weapons skills and partly endurance; fighting is very hard work and to become too tired can be fatal. But without cunning we'd have been destroyed. It's important to fight at an advantage. In the Ukraine we were careful always to fight them in the forest; we were no match for them on horseback. Now we are correcting that. Would you like to see warriors train on horseback?"

"Oh, yes!" Nikko answered. "I love horses and riding."

"I'll have someone take you tomorrow morning then. But now I'll show you your tent. It should be built by now, and I have things to do before the sun sets."

The tent frame had been set up—long saplings cut, bent, and lashed into the form of a tortoise. Several women and girls were covering it with hides. Temporary-looking and small, she thought, for someone who was temporary and alone.

"You will take your meals at the hut of Ulf Vargson," Nils told her. "Ulf is chief of the Wolf Clan. He has two daughters still at home, helping his wives, and they will be pleased to ask questions and answer yours."

She looked up at his strong well-balanced face. He couldn't be older than his mid-twenties, she decided, much younger than her own thirty-four years, yet somehow she reacted to him as her senior. There was something compelling about him, some inner difference beyond the telepathy and the sometimes disconcertingly direct intelligence.

"When will I talk to you again?" she asked. "There are so many things I'd like to know: about your travels, and the Psi Alliance, and Kazi."

Nils grinned at her, taking her by surprise, and in that moment he seemed like any large good-looking athletic youth. "I'll be back before dark. Ilse and I have a tent too, the cone-shaped one by the birch grove." He pointed. "I copied its form from the horse-barbarians. Come. I'll introduce you to Ulf's family."

Horse barbarians. That's another I'll have to ask about, she thought.

She felt impatient for the evening.

The broiled meat required strong chewing, and Nikko stopped eating not because she was full but because her jaws and cheeks could chew no more. No wonder these people have such strong faces, she thought; they develop a bite like a dire bear's. A congealed reddish pudding had also been served, which she decided not to ask about; if it was made with blood she preferred not to know yet. Her palate insisted it was partly curdled milk.

Conversation had gone haltingly. The girls, especially, kept forgetting to speak slowly and often had to repeat themselves. None of the family spoke any Anglic at all and there was no one to clarify words for either side. But an hour of this improved Nikko's ability noticeably.

Then Ulf raised his thick-shouldered form and stretched. "I have to sleep early tonight. I'll be training all day tomorrow, learning to fight in the saddle like a horse barbarian, and I'm not as young as I used to be."

"Ho! Listen to him," his principal wife said fondly. "I've seen him spar with a man half his age and make the young one dizzy with his sword play."

The chieftain laughed. "But the young ones can fight all day and make love half the night." He poked the woman playfully with an elbow. "I could too, when I was twenty. Now I need my sleep."

Nikko thanked them and left for her own tent a few dozen meters away. It was still daylight, but the sun had set. Inside the entrance dry wood had been stacked, along with birch bark for kindling. There was also a heap of leafy green twigs, its purpose unknown to her. Dry grass lay piled as a bed against one side, and she unrolled her light sleeping bag on it. Next she opened the small field chest and re-inventoried, then switched on the little radio and checked in with the *Phaeacia*, giving Matthew a resume.

That done, she left. She found Nils sitting cross-legged on the ground outside his door, his expression one of relaxed serenity, a young pagan god, blond and tan. It was dusk now, and mosquitoes were foraging in numbers but he did not seem to notice. Her hand snapped upward as she approached, smashing one on her forehead.

Nils stood and gestured her into his tent.

"Sorry," she said. "We have biting insects a lot like these on my world, but I'm not used to so many of them."

"I'll light a fire," he said. "They don't like smoke." He smiled. "You'll get used to them though, and they take very small bites. On warm still nights they were worse than this in the homeland." With flint and steel he quickly had a small wad of tinder glowing, blew it into a tiny fire and built it up with birchbark and branchwood.

"Will your people learn to like this land as much as the old?" Nikko asked.

"Most already like it better. It's a richer land, easier to live in, and very beautiful. We call the old land 'homeland' because of the memories and—" he groped momentarily—"traditions, but we are glad to be here."

The fire flamed briskly and Nils piled leafy twigs on it. The burning slowed and smoke billowed. He took two bundles of furs from the grassy bed oppo-site the entrance and set them near one another for seats.

"What would you like to hear about first?" he asked.

"One thing we'd especially like to know is what happened long ago that cut off travel from this world to ours, and why there are so few people on Earth today."

"Ah, the Plague. The tribes have only the word for it, and a few vague stories, but the Kinfolk—the Alliance—speak of it in detail and certainty."

Nils told her of an epidemic that had hit sud-denly, that the ancient healers could do nothing about and which spared only a scattered few. When someone sickened with it he was taken with a terrible urge to make fire, to burn things, and soon died. The cities reeked with smoke and rotting flesh, and before many days it was over. The few who survived could search for a day or more be-fore finding someone else alive. Soon the little moons that circled above the sky died because there was no one to take care of them, and when the little moons died, the machines died that had made life easy for men.

As he talked, her eyes searched his face, and whether he told of death and burning or of the gradual gathering and regrowth of mankind, his expression and voice remained casual. Yet he didn't seem uncaring, and his calm was due to more than remoteness of the events in time. It reflected some-thing in him that she had never known before.

"Are others of your people like you?" she asked. "Or other telepaths? Who think like you and look at things the way you do?"

"No," he said. "I do not know of any other who sees as I do, although Ilse is coming to."

"When did you become like you are?"

"Somewhat, I have always been. Then I killed the troll and was almost killed by it. When I woke up afterward, I knew."

"When you killed the *troll*?"

He nodded, and for a moment she was shaken, wondering if, after all, the difference in him was that he was insane. He laughed, she blushed, and he began to tell a story. It began with a boy, a sword apprentice in his eighteenth summer, who killed a man with a fist blow, was dubbed Ironhand, and exiled. A boy-man, naive, ignorant, but almost unmatched with the sword. At first things happened to him. Before long he happened to them. And there *were* trolls, which the chief of the Psi Alliance believed had been brought in ancient times from the stars.

She stared as he talked, her eyes growing full of him, exploring him, his smooth skin molded over muscles that were tiger-like in their power and grace, relaxed but explosive and possessed of more than human strength, ruddied by the settling fire. He turned his eyes to her, and suddenly her desire for him flashed into intense consciousness. She had shifted closer to him, unaware, and found herself leaning toward him. The realization jerked her upright, confused and frightened. Scrambling to her feet she scurried crouching through the low entrance into the night. She actually ran for a few meters, fought back the edge of panic and slowed to a walk, then stopped and looked around. It was dark and she could see no one. Her tent was over there, and she walked toward it, heart hammering. Had he hypnotized her? No. It had come from inside *her*, from within herself, an expression and surfacing of some deep inner response to him. She was still shaky, her pulse rapid from the shock and unexpectedness of it. She'd never imagined anything like that.

Inside her tent she opened the field chest. Humming mosquitoes were finding her in vicious numbers. She located the little battery lamp by feel, and with its soft white civilized light found the small cylindrical fire-lighter. She needed only to twist the top off, thumb the slide, and . . . She gripped it harder but still the top wouldn't turn; she gripped it as hard as she could, futilely. Using her handkerchief made no difference, and there were no pliers in the kit. "Damn damn damn," she gritted, then almost cried, and finally sat on her bed of grass, listening to the humming, feeling the stings.

After a minute's despondency she crawled outside again, walked slowly to Nils's tent, and ducked into its ember-lit interior. He still sat as he had, as if waiting.

"I can't light my fire," she said in a low voice.

He nodded silently, got up, and left with her. Side by side they walked through the darkness and entered her tent. She lit the small lamp again and he did not comment on it.

"If you could open this. . . ."

He held the small cylinder in his palm, looking at it, and it occurred to Nikko that he had never seen a screw cap before. But he knew. Gripping the top, he turned it easily, handed it back, and watched silently while she made a small rough pile of birch bark and twigs. In a moment she had a fire burning. At that he left, and she knelt for a few minutes, feeding the rising flames, then piled on leafy twigs as she'd seen Nils do.

She felt a sense of relief as the smoke diffused through the tent, and lay down in her jump suit atop the sleeping bag. Dark humor sparked briefly in her mind: I wonder if he'd have jumped and run if I'd reached for him. But the humor died. I'm no different than I was yesterday, she told herself. I just know something about myself I didn't know before. Now that I know, I won't be taken by surprise again.

Had he known before it surfaced? Then why had he gone on talking? But what else should he have done? Told her to get out before she made a fool of herself?

How many naked souls had he seen? What understanding must he have?

With that she felt better, but her mind would not be still. What would have happened if he'd reached out, put his hands on her, drawn her down onto the bed of grass? The thought requickened her pulse, tightening her throat; that was her answer. But he hadn't, and the sag of disappointment reinforced that answer. He could have but hadn't. Maybe the fact that she was older . . . but she was still quite pretty. She liked to look at her face in the mirror, and at her small neat figure.

Or perhaps he'd sensed the guilt she'd feel if she had had sex with him.

Were his reasons either of those or was she simply talking to herself? What mattered was that nothing physical had happened. She pictured Matthew's face then, and somehow the feeling that followed was of sober relief. Tension drained from her, and for a few minutes her thoughts were deliberately of years and dreams and tenderness shared, until she fell asleep with pungent smoke in her nostrils.

XI

Anne Marie zipped her jumper over her swim suit, then turned to the large window to look across city and prairie toward the sea.

"I wonder if there are sharks in the Black Sea?"

"Probably. It's hooked up with the Mediterranean and the world ocean. You know, these Earth sharks are a lot like sharks back home, even to the cartilaginous skeletons." Chandra looked at his watch. "No use making Matt wait," he said, reaching to the small radio.

"*Phaeacia*, this is Chan. *Phaeacia*, this is Chan. Over."

"Good morning, Chan. How's everything down on Planet Earth?" The voice was Matthew but the false heartiness wasn't.

Chandra raised an eyebrow at Anne Marie. "Just fine," he answered. "We plan to spend the day swimming and beach-combing along the Black Sea."

"Say, that sounds great! I should have given myself that job. Taking a picnic lunch too?"

There was an awkward lag before Chandra replied. "Matt, we're wasting our time here, and we've had our fill of it. How about pulling us out?"

"I don't think we want to do anything like that, Chan." There was a pause. "I'll tell you what I do want to do though. We're having a conference tomorrow of the whole exploration team, and I need you two to be in on it. Have the orcs bring you out to the landing spot at ten hundred local time tomorrow and we'll pick you up. That's the same spot we landed at before. At ten hundred hours. We'll have you back there twenty-four hours later."

"Sounds great, all but the last part. For all the good we're doing here, you'd have done better to leave us back on New Home."

"Okay, that's enough of that." Matthew sounded distinctly annoyed. "We all agreed that Constanta would be Contact Prime. You'll just have to stay with it down there until they trust you. You'll feel different about it then. So no more argument, okay?"

Anne Marie looked perplexedly at Chandra.

"Okay, Matt, you're the boss," he said. "Tomorrow at ten hundred hours local time and back the next day."

"Good." Matthew sounded mollified. "And Chan, no need to pack. Just leave your stuff there. But bring your radio with you so one of the technicians can go over it. It fades a bit now and then."

"Sure. Leave our personal gear and just bring the radio. Anything else, or should I sign off?"

"That's all for now. And no use checking in again unless you have something special to report. We'll see you tomorrow at ten hundred hours. And sorry I blew my top. Have a good time on the beach today, both of you."

"Sure thing. Chan over and out."

"Accepted. *Phaeacia* out."

Chandra stood up. "Huh! What did you think of that?"

"I don't know what to think of it. It was Matt's voice, but he certainly didn't sound like himself. He sounded—out of character. Do you suppose something's wrong up there and he doesn't want to tell us?"

Chandra pursed his lips and looked thoughtfully at his nails. "I'll tell you what, and I'll bet ten credits I'm right. He doesn't plan to bring us back here once he's gotten us away, and he doesn't want us to know it."

"But that doesn't make any sense," she objected. "Why wouldn't he want us to know? He knows we'd be overjoyed to hear it."

Chandra shrugged. "I've played cards with him; he's the world's most transparent faker. Think about it: The big hearty opening; that told me right away that he was going to withhold something from us. Then the big emphasis on coming back. His reaction when I suggested we shouldn't. You know what I think? I think he's decided these people are dangerous to us and he wants us out of here. And he thinks if we don't know it we'll act normal so the orcs won't suspect anything."

Anne Marie looked doubtful. "Well, I guess we'll find out for sure tomorrow. He did sound strange, there's no doubt about that."

Draco clapped his palms and the slave moved smoothly to refill his cup, reacting with neither expression nor thought to his ill humor. The consul had resented having to make a critical decision on nothing more than suspicion and supposition. The star man *supposed* they wouldn't return.

Well, he should know his commander.

And apparently Ahmed believed him. He'd proposed they not take the couple back to the sky chariot, but hold them hostage. They would threaten to torture them if a sky chariot, with weapons, wasn't given to them. They would promise to return the hostages as soon as they had delivery and had been shown how to drive it and use its weapons.

What particularly bothered Draco was that Ahmed wanted to meet the chariot when it landed tomorrow. That could prove dangerous and seemed totally unnecessary; they could use the hostage's "radio" to make their demands. But Ahmed had said he'd go alone if need be. He'd had the gall to imply that Draco might be afraid, and insisted it was the only way to know the star men's thoughts when they learned the situation. The reasoning was trivial—they didn't need to know their thoughts—and the Sudanese knew damned well he'd see through it.

Then, just a few minutes ago, Draco had been informed that, when the pair had been taken into custody, Ahmed's men had questioned them, had wanted to know how to enter a sky chariot if the invisible wall was not in place. A few screams from the woman had broken the man's refusal.

So the Sudanese dog planned somehow to capture the sky chariot tomorrow, unless this was a red herring covering still another intention.

It might be hard to counter Ahmed's plan without knowing what it was. The best thing to do, Draco decided, was to make a move of his own. At least he was forewarned. When they went to the landing place he'd be fully alert, ready to react quickly if necessary.

And while they were gone, his own people would strike down the men who guarded Ahmed's interest in the prisoners. Then they'd be solely *his* hostages, in his own dungeon. It was risky—Ahmed might even go to war over it—but he couldn't let Ahmed have the initiative alone.

His hostages. The thought excited him. The woman had screamed and then sobbed, when all they had done was jerk her arm up behind her back and twist it, and strike her in the abdomen once or twice.

Ahmed slipped his helmet on his proud head and was turning toward the courtyard when his spy entered, obviously with something to tell him.

"Make it quick!" he snapped. "I have no time for trivia now."

"In private, Lordship," the man said, and that in itself proved its urgency. Ahmed strode into his chamber, Yusuf and the spy with him, and closed the heavy bronze door, leaving his retinue behind.

"Speak!"

"Draco plans to have the man and woman taken for his own! It will be done as soon as you've left the city to meet the sky chariot."

The hardness in Ahmed's mood eased discernibly. "Good."

Yusuf's expression sharpened.

"Our move is risky," Ahmed explained. "Its success could seem to give us too great an advantage, and Draco might strike with his army immediately, before we could make use of it. His army is the stronger now. And if we kill him today, when perhaps we have a chance, his lieutenants would strike at once. He has been careful to give power to men who hate us as much as he does, and fear us more.

"But now he'll have his own coup." Ahmed jabbed the spy's shoulder painfully with a rigid finger. "You must see to it that he is *not* foiled. Our success today can be decisive in the long run only if there is a long run, while his will mean little except to his vanity. If he succeeds in this he'll be pleased with it, and unlikely to strike at us for awhile. By the time he sees its emptiness, it will be too late for him.

"Now let's get out of here." The heavy door was delicately balanced and opened easily at his pull. "We cannot be late."

It was a beautiful carriage, delicate-looking, incongruous on the prairie; it would have been more apropos in a fairy tale. Its erect oval body, completely enclosing, was an opalescent pearly white, like the magical egg of some fabulous bird. The ornate crown around its top was gold plated and its tall wheels marked with gold. The pair of light geldings pulled it almost as easily as they would a sulky, and its springs were so well made that it rocked only modestly at their walking pace, hardly bouncing as it crossed the prairie's humpy surface.

It was a parade carriage for captured royalty; its upper sides could be slid down for viewing prisoners. Had the detailed carvings of the crown been noticed by the men in the high-hovering *Alpha*, the triumphant depictions of butchery and rape might have shaken them.

Mikhail and Matthew were alone in the pinnace,

watching the view screen. "Trojan horse," Matthew muttered.

"How's that?"

"I said 'Trojan horse.' It occurred to me that that carriage down there is big enough to conceal several soldiers. Let's keep that in mind."

The carriage was on a different course to the landing site, a longer, smoother route, and Draco eyed it suspiciously. It was probably the key to Ahmed's scheme, though it might be nothing more than a ruse to hold the attention of those in the sky chariot, making them less likely to notice that the people in jump suits were not their people after all.

He looked them over. Ahmed had done a good job of selecting stand-ins; they were very close to the hostages in size and build. And the mellow brown of the star people's skins had been easy to match. But they . . .

And then he read what was in the carriage, his gaze jerking toward it in alarm.

Ahmed was intent, and perhaps more anxious then Draco. For him the point of no return was well past, and he knew how easily things could go wrong in this. If the star men waited to land until the party was close to the landing spot, as they had the last time, then the odds were good. Unless of course they discovered the substitutions before they landed. In that case he would be a dead man; they all would.

But if they landed too soon and activated the force shield, there'd be little he could do. That would almost surely mean failure, and also probably death.

                    *   *   *

They stopped at the base of the little hillock, twenty meters from where the pinnace had landed before, and watched the *Alpha* begin to settle. One orc, at the rear of the party, dismounted.

Seated at the front of the parade carriage, his mind screened, the telepathic driver strained briefly to sense the minds of the star men above. His hand was on the lever which controlled the side panels. The rods had been shortened. When the lever was pushed they would drop abruptly instead of lowering slowly.

He directed his attention, his and that of the arena troll enclosed behind him, to Ahmed's taut mind. His stomach was a clenched fist. His mind would hurt, as it had hurt in the arena when Kazi had held a troll's mind with his own and buffeted the cowering crowd with his rage. More. It would hurt as it had when the giant Northman, naked on the bloody sand, had torn the troll's mind away from the Master and slammed the throng into unconsciousness.

The sky chariot was almost down, and it would hurt badly.

"NOW!" Ahmed thought to him, and the panels dropped, and a burst of sheer rage and violence exploded from Ahmed into the troll's mirror mind. Instantly it burst back, greatly magnified, and Ahmed wasn't even able to clutch his stallion's mane before dropping like a sack from the saddle. Horses bolted at the thunderclap of psychic rage, or staggered and fell, and some of the unconscious party were dragged bouncing across the prairie. The *Alpha* landed with a bump, Matthew and Mikhail senseless on her deck.

The only man left conscious was the orc who'd dismounted earlier. He was that rarity, a man totally psi-deaf, selected by Ahmed for this job. The hard-bitten veteran swaggered to the pinnace, deactivated the lock, and within a minute had dragged two shackled bodies out into the tall grass. Then he squatted in the shadow of the *Alpha* to wait. It wouldn't be long. He could see the horsemen galloping toward him some distance away. They had been far enough off that the star men would not relate them to the landing, far enough that the thunderbolt from Ahmed's mind, magnified by the troll's, was a distant signal, not a felling blow.

There'd be a reward in this for him; perhaps he'd ask for a pretty slave girl from the palace household.

The squawk box was urgent. "Captain Uithoudt to the bridge please! Emergency! Captain Uithoudt to the bridge *please*! Emergency!"

Ram Uithoudt jabbed the acknowledge button, spit toothpaste into the washbowl, took a moment to rinse it down the drain, then pulled on his jumpsuit, zipping it as he strode down the passageway.

"The radio, sir," the bridge watch told him.

"Ram here," he said as he hit the command chair.

"Commander Uithoudt?"

The unfamiliar voice was quiet but hard, its words accented.

"That's right. Who are you?"

"I am Ahmed, consul of the Empire of Kazi. I have your, ah, pinnace in my control—the one called *Alpha*. I also hold prisoner the two men who flew it, Matthew Kumalo and Mikhail Ciano. I plan no harm to them, as long as you do not try to interfere with me. My fight is not with you. But if you try to interfere, their death will be your responsibility, and it will be a slow and most unpleasant death. I have experts at that.

"You will also leave your radio on at all times; I will want to contact you again."

Abruptly the signal ended. The two men on the bridge stared at one another.

XII

Each human instinctively and unconsciously develops the equivalent of computer programs in his mind—a set of more or less integrated and often incompatible programs that together crudely simulate the world. Your programs collectively constitute the world as you know it, and the state of those programs at any given time makes up the only world you know. They are the means through which your brain, your organic computer, operates. You make decisions and take actions on the basis of the printouts of that computer, printouts from programs which are part of your model of the world.[3]

Hendricks has discussed the deficiencies of the system at length.[4] Only one of them seems directly relevant to our discussion here—*the egocentricity of those programs.* The focal point, the emotional center, of the programs constituting your world, is occupied by your enthroned ego. It colors not only all you think and do, but all you "know" as well. It makes your subjective world what Kuznetsov dubbed the *ego world.*[5]

It has been suggested that this centrality of the

ego is essential as an integrating reference point and for survival of the organism; that without it, man would lack, among other things, a survival instinct.[6] The ego may indeed have begun as a reference point for the integration of data, and its growth may have been a by-product of the survival instinct, but it seems unessential to either. Descriptions and analyses of the barbarian telepath, Nils Järnhann, all point to his lack of an ego, as the concept of ego is defined today.[7] Yet even allowing for some small degree of exaggeration in the reports of the expedition, Nils did an exceptional job of integrating information and surviving remarkably hazardous situations.[8]

To be convincing, any refinement of ego theory must now consider Nils Järnhann. Which is to say, it must consider the probability of a strong and effective survival mechanism and an integrating center of reference independent of any powerful, albeit unconscious, emotional image of the self as the center of the world.

At the same time, of course, we must reject the "explanations" of the New Movement gnostics.[9] These are essentially pre-technological theology in pseudo-scientific trappings, with the unlikely premise that the human ego is the "spirit" or "soul" in a somehow degraded condition. Nils Järnhann, then, is "explained" as a case in which the degraded condition was somehow miraculously dispelled or perhaps avoided! . . .

. . . Operating with a set of seemingly objective programs, a non-egocentric world model, Nils showed unique ability to learn. Mrs. Kumalo found existing intelligence tests inadequate for precise determination, but established that he did in fact possess "substantially superior mental equipment."[12]

An alternative, or more likely complementary, explanation might be that his objectivity itself enabled him to discern, learn, and reason more effectively than the great majority of men.

Of course, his direct access to the thoughts of others must have helped, but most other telepaths seem not to approach him in ability to learn or to make correct decisions.

All in all there was that about him which makes one uncomfortable when trying to explain him scientifically. And that is entirely aside from the interesting apocrypha that have grown up about him. It seems as if he was playing a joke on us by being what he was.

Mrs. Kumalo questioned him in a specific effort to understand his gestalt (sensu Watanabe). She stated categorically that she never succeeded, but felt she could characterize certain aspects of it.[13] She wrote that, among other things, he did not have or use a conscious mind in the usual sense of the term. Yet he was obviously very conscious indeed. He was more sensitive to what happened around him, more aware, than anyone else she had ever known, an impression of him shared by the expedition generally.[14] Nor was he a cold hard logic machine—a biophysical computer so to speak. He has been described as cheerful, considerate of others, charismatic, and possessing a sense of humor,[15] which, to me at least, is reassuring.

Even more than with most men, the productive work of his mind apparently took place at a subconscious level. And he does not seem to have reviewed its "printouts" consciously. Whatever monitoring of them he may have done seems, like the computing itself, to have been subliminal. His printouts were available, however, for what we might call conscious expression. That is, he could explain his reasons better and more simply than most of us explain ours, and I suspect that if he were writing this, it would be much simpler and considerably more enlightening.

I can at least hope that if he were reading this, he would not laugh, and might even approve.

From—*Human Consciousness in the Light of the Barbarian Telepath, Nils Järnhann,* by Muhammad Chao. Pages 39-57, *in* ADVANCES IN PHILOSOPHY FOLLOWING THE FIRST TWO EARTH EXPEDITIONS. Kathleen Murti, ed. University Press, A.C. 867.

Nikko ducked into her tent and laid the armload of green-leaved willow twigs beside the firewood she'd brought earlier, then hung her canteen from one of the saplings that formed her tent frame. Her light field shoes were wet from the marshy ground where the willows grew. *So this is the simple life*, she thought. *Not bad, as long as someone else provides the food and prepares it. A lot more agreeable than the life Anne and Chan described in the palace.* The key difference, she decided, was the people.

As she took the radio from the field chest she wondered what Matthew would assign Chan and Anne to, now that they'd left the orcs, and whether contact with the orcs would be abandoned.

"*Phaeacia*, this is Nikko. *Phaeacia*, this is Nikko. Over. Over."

"Nikko, this is Ram. Over."

"Good morning, Ram. It really is morning here, you know. The sun is up, birds are singing—you should have heard their chorus about daybreak. 'Din' is a better word for it. I just finished my morning duties as a bearer of the wood and drawer of water. And my watch says oh-seven-oh-five local time, which makes it official. We had tough broiled meat again for breakfast, and my jaws are getting so strong I'll soon be able to hang from a rope by my teeth."

"Nikko, I've got something to tell you." He said it in a flat even tone of voice, cutting her communication, and it froze the breath in her chest. Fragments of thought splashed through her mind—Matt hurt in a pinnace crash; Ilse, her safeguard, dead in childbirth; something irreparable gone wrong with the space drive. She waited, not asking.

"Matt and Mike and the *Alpha* were captured by the orcs yesterday. We don't know how. I was afraid something was wrong when they didn't come back on schedule with Chan and Anne and we couldn't raise them on the radio. But we didn't know anything for sure, and I didn't want to alarm you when you checked in last evening.

"Not long after I talked to you I had a call from an orc headman named Ahmed. He said they had the *Alpha*, and Matt and Mike. He said they don't regard us as enemies and won't harm them as long as we do nothing to interfere. He didn't say what we shouldn't interfere in, but I guess we'll know when the time comes."

He paused. "I'll send *Beta* down with Ilse later today and bring you back up."

"No."

"No? What do you mean?"

"I mean no." She listened to her words as if someone else was speaking them. "I'd be no good up there to myself or anyone else, and everyone would be walking on tiptoe around me. Let me bring Nils to talk to you, if I can find him. He knows a lot about the orcs and might have something to offer—information or even advice. I'll switch off and be back as soon as I can, but I'm not sure how long it will be. Okay?"

"All right, Nikko, go ahead. But listen: After this don't use Band D anymore and watch for multiple receiver signals. We don't want eavesdroppers. *Phaeacia* over and out."

"Okay. Nikko out."

From high above, Ram heard her set go dead, and sat feeling grimly miserable. That was a hell of a fine woman. He wondered if it was true that, in a pinch, women were likely to be tougher than men. And he wondered about Anne and Chandra. The man named Ahmed hadn't mentioned them. They must be prisoners too. There was hardly anything else they could be, except dead.

Nikko walked swiftly to Nils's tent. He wasn't there. She turned toward Ulf's then, and he was gone too. Nikko explained, and the principal wife sent her youngest son, a boy of nine, pelting off to look for Nils.

"He'll ask other boys," she said, "and before long there'll be a small army hunting for him. If he's anywhere near, he'll hear their minds; it shouldn't take long. Why don't we go to your tent and wait for him?" She put a large strong hand on Nikko's shoulder while giving instructions to the youngest wife. Then they left.

They sat down on the ground beside Nikko's tent. "It's natural to feel afraid," the woman said. "But if your man is still alive, he may get back all right. And if he doesn't, it will pass. You are still young and pretty. Not strong-bodied, but pretty none the less. Any man would be glad to take you into his cabin. Besides, you star people have sky boats, and ancient weapons to threaten the orcs with. Nils will know what to do. Even the chiefs turn to the Yngling for his wisdom."

They sat in silence then, Nikko's mind curiously calm. To the south rose the ridge that bordered the valley, at that distance looking more black than green. Along its crest she could distinguish the tops of individual pines and firs, small against the sky. The omnipresent smell of wood smoke was around her, but beneath it were the subtler fragrances of meadow flowers. And there was birdsong. She felt high and strong and sure—not afraid at all—and while she knew the feeling would prove transient, that was all right too. She was enjoying it now.

When Nils arrived she arose with composure, and the principal wife left. Nikko told him what Ram had said. Then they went into the tent and she recontacted the ship.

"This is Ram. Over."

"Nils is here, Ram. Ilse's husband. He's a member of the War Council and an advisor to the Council of Chiefs—sort of an affiliate member. He speaks Anglic well."

"Okay," Ram said. "Do you have questions to ask him, or how will we handle this?"

"Why not just have him say whatever comes to him? If any questions come to my mind, he'll know. He's a telepath." She handed the microphone to the Northman, who held it as if he used one every day.

"Tell me what the orc said, as exactly as you can," Nils instructed.

When Ram was done, Nils took over. "Kazi ruled when I was there, and I don't know this Ahmed. But you can be sure he's cruel. No man could rule the orcs who was not cruel and ruthless."

You bastard, Ram thought, *did you have to say that? In front of her?*

"He may be more sane than Kazi though," Nils continued, "and therefore perhaps more predictable. And it sounds as if he wants something more from you. That's hopeful for the hostages, for now. But when he asks for more, you'll have to make some answer. To say 'no' will put the hostages in danger, but 'yes' may not be an answer you can give. Prepare yourself for that.

"In deciding your answer, remember that orcs love torture, and they are masters at it. They know how to torture the mind as well as the body . . ."

And so do you, thought Ram, *you barbarian son of a bitch.*

". . . and when a hostage has served his purpose, they may use him to amuse themselves. Unless of course they're afraid to, afraid of heavy vengeance. You might make a show of force, to make them fear you. But warn them first, so they don't think they are being attacked and perhaps kill their captives. Don't threaten them; just show them what you can do. Attack a herd of cattle.

"They know a lot about you from the minds of your people. Undoubtedly they have decided you are weak-willed."

Thanks a lot.

"Show them they're wrong and they'll become more cautious.

"They already have a sky boat"—Nils paused momentarily, catching Nikko's unspoken correction, "a pinnace, with its weapons, so their need for hostages is less than it would be otherwise, and they may be more willing to kill them. It would be much better if you could get the pinnace back. Maybe we could do that for you. If you would take a party of our warriors in the other pinnace, perhaps we could get it back for you."

Yeah, Ram thought. *Then you'd have both* Alpha *and* Beta, *the orcs would still have four of us, and we'd have nothing to bargain, or even land, with.* Instead he answered, "We can't do that. First of all we don't know where the *Alpha* is. We reconnoitered first thing this morning and couldn't find a trace of her. They've either got her under cover in the city or they keep her somewhere well outside it. And second, if they're as bad as you say—and it fits what Chan and Anne thought—they might retaliate against the hostages if we try to get *Alpha* back that way."

Nikko reached out and Nils handed her the microphone.

"What do you have in mind then, Ram?"

"Nothing. I hate to say it, but not a damned thing. We'll just have to wait and see what develops, and take advantage of any opportunities."

She looked at Nils but his face told her nothing.

"Are you sure you won't come back up?" Ram asked. "We'd feel better if you were here, and you'd know at once if we hear anything."

"You won't," she answered softly. "Nothing good. Nothing good will happen unless we make it happen."

Five hundred and ten kilometers above her, Ram's expression was dismal.

"No, I'll stay here," she continued. "I'll be doing what we came here to do. Up there all I could do would be wait and imagine and feel sick and afraid. But thanks, Ram. And I know if there's anything you can do, you will. Nikko over and out."

"Accepted. *Phaeacia* out."

Ram stared at the colored image in the big screen, a broad span of Eurasia tan and white, the Black Sea's cobalt blue, unmarked by clouds. "Welcome home," he said bitterly. "Welcome back to Earth."

Nils sat on a fallen tree in the forest, head bowed, thick forearms resting on powerful thighs. He wore a loin cloth like a horse barbarian. Sten Vannaren stood over him intently, razor in hand, now and then hissing slightly between his teeth.

Nils had made a decision. The probability of full success was not high, but he saw no real alternative.

The orcs had a pinnace, with weapons and a supply of ammunition. Nils had gathered a substantial picture of what could be done with them. And with a combination of questioning, telepathy, psychology and pain, the orcs would soon know how to use them. Then they'd be able to: (1) attack and harass the People; (2) prevent effective cattle raids; and (3) scatter the herds the People had already gathered. They could force the clans to disperse and leave the country. Furthermore, if they could coerce the star people to provide additional ammunition, which was likely, they might well try again to seize Europe, using extortion, war, and potential allies among short-sighted, opportunistic feudal lords.

The best chance of preventing this, perhaps the only chance, was to get control of the *Beta*. If they could recapture *Alpha* with it, success would be almost assured. But just getting *Beta* would improve the odds. When the time came they'd attempt it by holding Nikko hostage. The star people seemed psychologically unable to retaliate by harming Ilse. He had advised Kniv, and Axel Stornäve, not to give the star woman up if she decided after all to go back to the ship.

Now he would try to find where *Alpha* was kept.

Sten stepped back and grinned at Nils's newly bald head. "There! It's done. And without drawing too much blood. It'll be a long time before it grows out enough to braid again." He folded the razor and put it in his pouch. "Are you sure you don't want a man or two beside you in this? That crazy Trollsverd would cut *his* hair for the chance, maybe even his throat. And if you talked hard enough you might get me to go."

Nils grinned back at him. "Fighting isn't the purpose of this trip, and one Northman is hard enough to conceal among foreigners. Two or three would be impossible. Besides, you speak Anglic; I want you to keep Nikko happy. Answer her questions, talk freely, tell her your travels. She'll be learning, which is her purpose, and more content to stay, which means the star people will be less angry at us when the time comes. Talk to Ulf about having her take meals with your family. Once they know her, Signe and Hild won't be jealous when you spend time with her, especially if it's with them by their own fire.''

The two warriors shook hands then, untied their reins from the hazel bushes, and swung onto their horses. Sten turned back toward the encampment. Nils rode south.

XIII

Psionocists regard Ilse as the human cornerstone of psionics in the new renaissance. Her students remember and revere her as the calm, charismatic, and knowing listener who helped them find new dimensions within and outside themselves. Sean O'Niall insists that, in other times and circumstances, a new religion would have grown up around her memory,[31] and indeed one might wonder if one hasn't. Increasingly, philosophers recognize her as a major cultural transmuter, one whose unique insights and influence are moving mankind a step farther toward what we will become.[32]

It is interesting to consider that she was a very primitive young woman on a primitive and often violent world. The neoviking composer of the *Järnhann Saga*, in one of the occasional departures from his usual meter that provide a parenthetical quality, gives us a sharp clear image of the young Ilse in action while describing her capture by horse barbarians in Germany. He may well have exercised his culturally conditioned imagination, but the characterization seems basically correct. Here is the original, for those who can read it, along with Professor Kumalo's faithful translation.[33]

> D' döjtsa häxen käste ned
> böjen, näpte bågen upp
> å spennte senan, önar stadi,
> pilan vjentanne mä fäädi döjn.

> [The German seeress threw aside
> her bucket, quickly took her bow
> and drew the string taut, cool eyes steady,
> arrow waiting then with ready death.]

From—ROOTS OF THE NEW MOVE-
MENT, by Mei-Ti Lomasetewa

Dr. Celia Uithoudt stepped into the little cabin. "Ram?"

"What?" He responded without looking away from the tape screen.

She looked at her husband thoughtfully before continuing. "Did you read my mind just now?"

"You know I can't do that at will." He turned to her. "Why do you ask?"

"Because you sound grumpy—like a refusal waiting for a request. I thought maybe you knew I was going to ask you to do something."

"I guess maybe I did. Do what?"

"Talk to Ilse."

"What point is there in that?"

"Courtesy, if nothing else." For those four words her tone had sharpened. Now it softened again, but the words were candid. "Ram, you should know what the point is without being told. With Matt gone, you've undertaken to direct the off-ship activities as well as the ship itself. And Alex is willing to let you, even though he was Matt's second, because he's not the command type and doesn't feel up to the circumstances. And because you're willing and he has respect for your . . ."

"And you don't like the way I'm handling things," Ram interrupted roughly. "Maybe you ought to try it."

"Let me finish talking, you sarcastic bully!"

Her burst of open anger startled Ram, even shocked him. She seldom argued, rarely criticized bluntly, and he'd never seen her blow up before. He respected and appreciated her patience even more than her intelligence. To have broken that patience alerted him to how badly the situation had affected his frame of mind.

At a deeper level she had jabbed a hidden sore of self-distaste. He sometimes did use sarcasm to bully her, and despised this trait of his.

"Sorry, Cele," he said quietly. "I'll listen."

She stood uncomfortably for a wordless moment, her anger gone. "If you're going to make the decisions," she said at last, "you need to know as much as possible about the people and circumstances you're dealing with. And Ilse is a storehouse of information. She may seem like a primitive—I guess she is, in one sense of the word—but she's from a pretty wise culture. The Kinfolk have kept alive quite a bit of the old knowledge. They're scattered throughout feudal Europe and keep one another more or less informed of what goes on there. They're sophisticated politically and they've been influencing feudal politics and culture for generations, so they have a lot better feel for intrigue and conflict than we do. They've retained a lot of twenty-first-century objectivism and rationalism, too, and on top of that she's learned a lot about the Northmen and at least something about the orcs.

"Besides, with your occasional periods of telepathic sensitivity, you might find it interesting to know a trained and highly functional telepath."

"You're right," he said. "And I will talk to her. I guess I let my frustrations get me down."

She bent and kissed her seated husband on the forehead.

"I've never seen you so impressed by anyone before," he went on. "Certainly not on just a few days' acquaintance."

"Don't let the greasy deerskin breeches mislead you," Celia said. "Besides, I've had some things sewn together for her, a bit lighter and easier to clean. She's too pregnant for any of our jumpsuits.

"You'll be impressed with her too, I promise. She's not only highly intelligent and magnetic, but she seems so, so *integrated*. When I talk with her I feel positively—outclassed—and you know inferiority isn't part of my self image."

Ram shook his head.

"Listen, Cele," he said. "For whatever it's worth, I apologize for being such a lout. Introduce me to Ilse. I've barely met her, and I need you to start me out. I hope she's used to people that run off at the mind. I can usually control my mouth, but . . ."

Cele had been right: magnetic was the word. And striking, almost handsome. On New Home, with its centuries of racial blending, her honey-blond hair and high color would have drawn immediate attention. But her real impact was of strength and composure. Even advanced pregnancy failed to make her seem weak or vulnerable. Yet she was very much a woman—swollen but physically attractive. And the sense of presence she radiated had affected Ram before she'd said a word.

He'd been surprised at her Anglic. On New Home, with its cultural conservatism and literary tradition, the language had not changed much, but he wouldn't have expected so little change in it on Earth. The Psi Alliance had kept it as their primary language, she explained. It helped maintain unity among the farflung members.

They'd nurtured it also among the people around them as a second language understood almost everywhere in feudal Europe. The Merchant Kin and the powerful Inner Circle had been instrumental in establishing Anglic among the upper classes, where the advantages of an international language maintained it. The monastic "Wandering Kin" had even kept it alive, if not exactly vigorous, among the peasantry. A deliberate policy of linguistic homogeneity, plus a strong oral and literary tradition, had kept it largely unchanged for more than seven hundred years.

And Ram could not doubt her telepathy. For the most part she waited for him to voice his questions and statements, but she'd openly anticipated him several times.

Although they did not seem pertinent to his problem, Ram found the Kinfolk especially interesting. "Do you mean to say," he asked, "that there are hundreds of psis in Europe forming a complete and intercommunicating culture and the populace as a whole doesn't know it?"

She nodded. "They know of the Wandering Kin

of course, but they don't realize what they are. The peasants regard them as seers and counselors, and look to them for advice, and that is as close as anyone comes to understanding them. Members of the Merchant Kin and the Inner Circle are thought of simply as shrewd individual merchants or advisors."

"And the Northmen don't know either?"

"Only Nils does; they have known of telepathy for only a few years. They were isolated for a long time in their northern land, and the Kinfolk have never been among them."

"What do they think of telepathy?"

"Their Yngling is a telepath, so they accept it. And it's their nature not to fear the new and unfamiliar. They have great confidence in their resourcefulness, their ability to handle whatever comes up. They may reject something as undesirable, but not from fear of its strangeness."

"You said their—something. Their Ingling? What's an Ingling?"

"Many of them believe my husband, Nils, is the Yngling. Long ago 'yngling' simply meant a youth in their language. Anciently, Anglic had a cognate, 'youngling.' All three Northman tribes share a legend of a young man, an yngling, who appeared in a time of danger perhaps three hundred years ago, when constant warring threatened to destroy them. They had no warrior class then; all men fought. The southern tribe, the Jötar, had gained the upper hand. It seemed they would kill or enslave the Svear, and perhaps the Norskar as well. But an yngling appeared among the Svear who became a great raid leader and war chief, and before long it seemed they would destroy the Jötar instead. Then an yngling came among the Jötar and saved them. Soon he made himself known as the same yngling who had saved the Svear and Norskar. He said he belonged to no tribe or clan, but to all Northmen. And he had great power over them by his wisdom and truth and justice, and gave them the bans that set limits on warring and feuding, the bans that let them live as men without fear and hate.

"But the yngling was killed by a Jytska chief who did not want to change, who hated him for the bans and struck him with a poisoned knife. And instead of making a burial mound, they put the body in a canoe and set it on the Jöta Älv, which floated it down to the sea.

"Only then they realized that no one in all the clans knew his name, so they called him the Yngling. After that it was no longer used as a word, but reserved to be his name. And it was widely held that if the tribes were ever in such need again, he would be reborn. A year ago the need was great, and Nils, who had been exiled earlier for a killing, returned and led them through their danger. So many of the People believe he is the Yngling."

An interesting bit of folklore, Ram thought. "And from what you said a bit ago," he commented, "I gather that all you know about the orcs is what he's told you."

"Not exactly; I have it by more than telling. He can re-picture things just as he experienced them, when he wishes. So he has rerun most of the time among the orcs for me to see, and hear and feel. It is much like having been there as him."

"Feelings and all! Do you experience them as

the participant, or do you retain your separate identity with feelings of your own?"

"I perceive his feelings but remain myself."

"Has it been hard to adjust to Northman customs and thoughts?" he asked. "After all, your own people are much more advanced."

She smiled slightly. "All my life many ways of thinking have been exposed to me. And knowing Nils, experiencing him, has changed me. I am much like he is now. I know as he knows."

And what was that like, Ram wondered? Was she losing her identity? Becoming a female mental reflection of a sweaty telepathic warrior? *I know as he knows. As,* not *what.* But it was himself she looked at now, seeing into his mind as if his skull were glass, his thoughts a reading tape. The realization embarrassed Ram, not because of his exposure but because she might be offended by what he'd been thinking.

Her eyes and mouth joined in smiling, and he felt relief.

"Ram," she said, "I believe you're the only one of your people on this ship who has meaningful psi potential. Perhaps I can teach you to use it, if you'd like."

"What did you think of her?" Celia asked.

"Pretty remarkable. Damned remarkable. Thanks, Cele, for pushing me. She's not only a walking reference library; she's going to train my psi potential."

"I thought you found your occasional flashes of telepathy painful—wished you didn't have them."

"You know the background, the reason for that. But it's like having sight and keeping your eyes closed; I need to face up to it now, to what I am and can be."

His expression changed. "Would it bother you, Cele, if I became a functional telepath?"

"I can't be sure. You're—not always nice, Ram, and I don't know how it would be, not being able to keep secrets from you. But I think you ought to do it. We'll work things out later if we need to."

He looked at her soberly for a moment. "Good," he said quietly. He kissed her gently on the corner of her mouth where it nestled against the smooth curve of her cheek. "I guess I better go to the bridge now."

XIV

The *Alpha* skimmed swiftly up the narrow valley sixty meters above the ground, began braking at the first sight of huts, slewed in a tight 360 degree turn above them while angling upward to a hundred meters, then moved upvalley again, but slowly now. Had Nikko seen it, she'd have known that none of her people were piloting. It had been flown with a hard arrogant snap.

She didn't see it though, only heard the alert as she knelt beneath the pines, helping Hild rake tubers from a fire before a lean-to. A sentry had spotted the pinnace and blown a signal on his great ox horn, a signal repeated in a series up the valley.

Her face tightened. There had been little doubt it would happen. Now it had. And she was afraid neither Matt nor Mike had given in easily.

Alpha continued up the line of clan encampments. Hard eyes scanned the landscape, finding no one. No one ran into the huts or from them. No one fled into the forest. No smoke rose from the roofs. She swooped parabolically to 2,500 meters, and a hairy brown hand adjusted the visual pickup. Then they drifted back down the valley.

There could be no question; the Northmen had abandoned their camps. They probably hadn't gone far though. There were hints of smoke, as of campfires, above the canopy of the timbered ridges, though nothing justifying the expenditure of ammunition.

With a jerk of acceleration the pinnace shot toward the valley mouth. They still would go home blooded. They would disperse the herd of Northman cattle they'd seen on the prairie beside the forest's edge, and shoot up the herdsmen, before returning to the city.

XV

An endless undulating sea of grass, the prairie dried beneath a towering sun. A caravan crept across its vastness, raising a train of dust to mark its passage. Carts and wagons, grinding drought-baked ruts and clods to flour, lurched and jolted clumsily, their teamsters swaying more or less awake. Armed guards rode beside the wagons, spitting gray grit, cursing the lack of breeze, cursing the merchants whose pay had brought them here, cursing their fellows who rode as scouts or flankers away from the choking dust.

Milio Gozzi shifted his bulk fruitlessly in the silver-inlaid saddle and thought of his younger brother who sat at home envying his wealth. Envying at home on a cushioned chair, fanned by a servant, tended by a lovely girl-mistress eager for position, a girl with young breasts like lemons and small dimpled hips.

He shifted again and grunted. Wealth grew only partly from shrewdness. It also required will, the exercise of correct judgment, and attention to details.

Seldom, but occasionally, he wished *he* was the

younger brother. Eat as one might, riding in the hot sun for long days was to feel the fat melt from one's bones, trickling down over sensitive skin to gather and turn to butter in the loosening creases around the torso, marinating and stinking. The worst was behind and the worst was ahead. The mountains had been more dangerous, sheltering bands of brigands, but the days of open steppe ahead promised to be hotter and dustier.

It was hard to make an honest credit today. Since the orcs had lost their emperor, the peace had not been kept as well. Brigands had grown bolder, forming larger, more ambitious forces. His escort was three times as large as in years past, and cost ten times as much, because the danger was greater and because he would keep them all the way to the City. In other years the orcs had not allowed an armed escort to come more than a day's ride past the mountains. Nor had it been necessary. Now bandits had attacked even farther out than this, it was said—two full days beyond the foothills. And it was rumored that barbarians had come into the country from a land of ice, infesting the mountains farther north and riding out to attack orc patrols!

One could hear anything, of course, but even lies often had roots in truth. The most disturbing evidence was that they had been advised to bring their escort to the City.

No one had encountered Northmen this far south yet. Gozzi laid a fat fist on the hilt of his short sword. He had no wish to be the first.

He squinted back along the string of wagons at the grimy toughs who rode in the dust, some with lances, some with bows, all with a shield slung

alongside and a sheathed sword. A band of surly
cut-throats who rode guard instead of raiding only
because the pay was surer and because the orcs
hunted brigands. They'd fought well though, that
time below the pass.

Some rode shirtless. It would be better if they
kept their mail on, but he did not press the issue.
He'd lost several in the fight and couldn't afford
desertions.

The caravan master pulled his black Arabian
alongside Gozzi. It was Gozzi's caravan and Gozzi
had hired him. The other merchants were lesser
men who'd paid to join their wagons with Gozzi's.

"Padrone," he said, pointing toward the sun, "it
is midday, and there's a creek just ahead. It would
be a good place to stop."

Gozzi nodded and the man jogged his horse down
the long train of wagons, calling instructions. When
the first wagon reached the stream, the caravan
stopped. Teamsters unhitched their horses and
walked them in harness to drink below the trail.
No fires were lit; they cooked at dawn and again
at evening, but lunch was quick and cold.

The mercenaries ate together in a loose cluster
of small groups, all but the outriders, joking and
gibing in Anglic as best they could, for their own
languages varied from Greek to Slovak, from
Catalan to Croat. They believed themselves better
than teamsters because they were more deadly
and better paid. They considered themselves better than the merchants for half the same reasons,
but kept it to themselves because they could not
trust one another.

As they ate and talked, they paid little attention
to what went on nearby. Vigilance was the duty of

outriders; their own job was to discourage raiders by their presence, and to fight if need be.

Milio Gozzi, on the other hand, was alert by disposition and practice. As he chewed, his eyes in their creases followed a man trotting his horse toward them from the east. Nudging the caravan master, he motioned with his head.

"I haven't seen that one before. Who is he?"

"I don't know," the man answered after a few seconds. "He's not one of ours."

The personal guards of the merchants rose to their feet.

A giant, thought Gozzi, and a resourceful one to have gotten past the outriders. The man dismounted four-score meters away, as if to reassure them, and led his horse, a stallion built to carry weight. Like a Turk, he wore only a breechclout in this season, though the merchant's shrewd eyes knew he customarily wore more. His legs were tanned less deeply than his torso, and neither was as dark as his face, while his stubbly scalp was flaking from recent sunburn.

He looked as powerful as his horse.

The giant wasted no time. "I'm looking for hire as a fighting man."

Gozzi wasn't surprised. His eyes had noted the line of sword callus on the man's right hand, like a ridge of horn from thumb to the end of the index finger, better developed than he had ever seen before. As for scars, he wore an ugly one on his left thigh, probably from an arrow, plus a trivial crease on the right bicep, but nothing more. Either he was inexperienced or very good, and the merchant was willing to bet that he was very good indeed.

"I've never heard that accent before," Gozzi said. "Where are you from?"

"From Svealann, a country of broad forests and great fighters." He grinned when he said it.

Gozzi sucked his upper lip thoughtfully. "Never heard of it," he said. "Suppose I tell you I have all the men I need?"

"One seldom has too many really good men. And you have one less man than you broke camp with this morning."

"You killed one of my men?"

The stranger shrugged. "He attacked when I only wanted to ask a question. And consider: I've saved you his pay and brought you a better man to replace him."

"One of the others still should have spotted him before he got this far," the caravan master said.

"And might have, if I'd been an armed band. But there are many low places where the grass grows tall, and my horse lies down on command. And perhaps your scouts were thinking about other things."

"You're hired," Gozzi said abruptly. "But not as an outrider. Outriders must be men you trust." He nodded to the caravan master. "He will ride beside the wagons."

Except to water the horses, the caravan didn't stop again until the sun was low in the west.

"Svealann? Never heard of it." The speaker was a smallish sinewy man with a short brown beard parted on the left cheek and jaw by a scar. "They must grow them big there."

"Some big, some small."

"And you're one of the little ones?"

The group of mercenaries broke into loud laughter.

Nils smiled easily. "I'm big in any company. Bigger in some than in others."

"What do you mean by that?"

The tone was belligerent. The man who asked was almost as tall as Nils, with shoulders muscled nearly to his ears. An outrider, he'd been scowling since they had made camp and he'd first seen the newcomer. Tražja had always been the biggest, wherever he was, and the strongest, and he had always dominated, from his first service as a mercenary when he'd been but seventeen.

Nils shrugged, and his very nonchalance antagonized the big Montenegrin. "Here!" Tražja held out his waterbag. "It's empty! Fill it!"

Nils said nothing, and did not reach to take it. The command combined insult and threat, and there was something eerie about his utter lack of reaction to either. His smile did not fade nor widen nor go stiff; he seemed truly as relaxed as before.

"I am the overman here," Tražja insisted, and shook the waterbag for emphasis.

"The caravan master is boss," Nils answered. "He said nothing to me about any other."

Tražja's lips pursed with anger and his eyes became slits. "I am the overman among us by my strength, not by the say of some master. Ask any of these." He motioned slightly with his head. "Ask any of them to deny I am the overman."

The men watched bright-eyed with anticipation, saying nothing.

"Then tell one of them to bring your water."

With an angry snarl, Tražja flung the leather bag at Nils's chest. "Fill it!"

Nils's posture changed slightly and his head

moved with a small deliberate negative. When Tražja pounced, the blow that met him was quick but heavy; he dropped to the ground and did not move. The others stared, stunned at the sudden totality of it.

Nils bent, picked up the waterbag and held it out to another man. "Fill it for him," he ordered. The man took it and trotted away toward the creek.

"You'd better kill him," said the smallish man with the brown beard, nodding toward Tražja. "He'll knife you now if he gets the chance."

Nils shook his head. "Not him. He'd never knife a man from behind or in his sleep. If he tries to knife me it will be from the front, and with warning. That's the kind of man he is."

The caravan park was at the west edge of the City. Drivers and mercenaries stretched awnings beside the wagons, cursed the lack of other shade, and waited for Gozzi to find out whether or not they would be allowed to go into the City. They'd all heard how merchants were entertained there, and while none seriously imagined such things would happen to them, they hoped to find taverns and houses where exceptional experiences might be met.

They watched the merchants talking with two orc officers and their accountants, and cursed the waiting and the thirst. Finally they saw the bulk of Gozzi walking toward them, the caravan master at his side.

Gozzi knew mercernaries and did not deny them needlessly. So he told them the simple truth and let the orc reputation do the rest. They were free, he reported, to walk about the City as they wished.

But there were no taverns, none at all, and they were to enter no building. Also, they were forbidden to carry weapons. A foreigner found with even a small knife would be arrested, and there was nothing anyone could do for him then except to wish him a quick death. If they chose to enter the City they would have to depend on the street patrols for protection. But the orc officers had said frankly there was a good chance they'd be attacked by playful soldiers when no patrol was nearby.

Gozzi promised, however, to see if liquor and girls could be sent to them. He did not actually intend to ask about liquor. Alcohol and idle mercenaries were an imprudent mixture in a place like this.

Nils awoke when he'd intended. The lopsided moon had descended to about twenty degrees above the horizon. He rolled out of the light sleeping robe, rose, and walked casually but silently toward one of the enclosed sleeping wagons used by the merchants, parked somewhat away from the freight wagons.

Ottoro, companion and clerk to one of the merchants, slept alone tonight while his master was in the City. He awoke in near blackness to a large hand over his mouth, and his eyes bulged with fright until he remembered his promise. He nodded, was released, sat up and felt for his ink pot and quill, then ducked through the rear door. The giant mercenary squatted in the edge of the shadow, moonlight on his calm face, and carefully Ottoro inked five numerals on the man's forehead.

When it was done the man stood, gripped the clerk's thin shoulders in silent thanks, and left.

Ottoro watched him out of sight among the shad owed freight wagons, and shivered. He didn't know what the giant had in mind but sensed it wa dangerous. And he didn't want him to die—tha magnificent animal body, those calm eyes. He wa the only one of the mercenaries that Ottoro wasn afraid of, the only one that neither leered no sneered. The man had spoken to him but once, t ask this favor, yet Ottoro felt stricken at the though he might never see him again.

Nils took a small bundle from his kit, strod quietly to the nearby latrine and sat cross-legge in the shadow behind it until the moon had se Then silently he slipped through the blackness out of the area and through a night-filled street t a nearby warehouse. Beneath a ramp he lay down He'd waken again at dawn, or sooner if there wa need.

In the warehouse district Nils was less conspicu ous than might be expected; many warehouse slave were large powerful men. In other respects the resembled most male slaves, with shaven scalp tattooed foreheads, and unbleached cotton tunic Slump-shouldered, expressionless, he had passe or circled every warehouse and granary on th riverfront before midmorning. Eyes, ears, and tel pathic sense had been alert for any clue that *Alph* was concealed in one of them. She wasn't, and h felt she hadn't been.

The arena seemed a possibility. Some of th beast pens might be large enough to hide a pinnac If it wasn't there, he would try the warehouses the harbor.

Nils walked faster now, and before long glimpse

the palace through a cross street. The pinnace might also lie beneath an awning on one of its numerous roofs. He remained intent, scanning for clues.

The four orcs had just turned a corner when they noticed him ahead.

"Look at that," one said pointing. "No slave ought to be that big. There's no one in the whole cohort that big."

"Yeah. Maybe we ought to shorten him."

"Which end?"

"How about the middle?"

They laughed.

"Now listen, you dog robbers," one of them warned, "take it easy. The brass has been getting mean about crippling slaves."

"That's right," said another. "Don't cut off anything that's any good to anyone."

They laughed again.

Although they were forty meters behind him, Nils had sensed their attention, and in a general way their intentions. He started diagonally across the broad street, not speeding up but heading now for the palace. Soldiers were unlikely to make a disturbance on the palace grounds. But the orcs had no reason to keep their pace slow, and they gained on him, grinning, their strides eager.

"Doesn't look like a eunuch."

"Not yet."

Their laughter was husky with anticipation. Nils sensed how near they'd drawn. He'd never reach the palace without running, and running would draw deadly attention. He turned through a doorway. Had it been a barracks, he might possibly have been safe, for no one might have been there, and his pursuers would not have invaded the territory of a different cohort. But they recognized it as a building housing female slaves! It was unbelievable that the big bastard would do that; only orcs had freedom of entry.

The first two followed him in quickly. Nils, standing against the wall beside the door, struck the second, his heavy-bladed knife entering below the ear. There was a choking gasp, and the man's partner, turning, had his ribs stove in by a calloused heel. A third orc blocked the doorway, pulling at his sword, then pitched backward, doubled, down the low steps. Nils emerged after him, with a sword now, and the fourth orc roared to see the slave cleave the fallen man. Very briefly they fought. When the man went down, Nils fled, while other shouting orcs ran toward him. Two blocked his way, then jumped aside when he didn't stop, following in pursuit when he was past. He turned a corner and the palace lay across a square. Tossing the sword away he sprinted hard, dodged between two groups of slaves, then stopped abruptly in their lee.

Before him stood a street patrol, staring, nocking arrows or leveling pikes. The hard-faced officer with the small deadly smile was a telepath. His eyes were intent on Nils's sweaty face with its numbers blurred and running as black rivulets down his face.

Quickly Nils threw off the tunic, to stand barbaric and proud in his breechclout, at the same time holding a clear mental picture of himself in the arena. If the telepath recognized him, he'd hardly have him killed on the spot.

The man barked a command and the patrol moved to encircle Nils. Angry soldiers were run-

ning up, and the officer shouted at them, his
voice dangerous, commanding. They sheathed their
swords, flushed and indignant, then stood at attention while he questioned them. More orders were
barked. Nils was manacled, and a pike prodded
his ribs. Accompanied by two of Nils's pursuers,
the patrol marched toward the palace.

XVI

The dire bear crawls obscenely from the tower
to haunt the involuted caves of night,
feeding on fear and love and tenderness,
ravening the vulnerable flesh
and quivering mind.

"Take me, take me instead!" I cry, but goes
shambling and chuckling in the darkness
out of sight with someone else.

And all the pores inhale
the terror of the unimaginable,
imagining.

From—EARTH, by Chandra Queiros

He had been to his cell, looked him over carefully, considered his aura, and questioned him. There could be no doubt: it was the same barbarian the Master had been interested in, who'd fought in the arena and escaped. Apparently the same man who'd killed the Master in single combat months later and a thousand kilometers away. He was thought to be a chief among his people.

Draco ground his fist on the cushioned arm of his chair. There must be a way to profit from such a catch. What bargain might be made with the Northmen? Perhaps the man was not a major chief. But he must be—one who could do what he had done. He felt dangerous even in a cell with chains on ankles and wrists.

Less dangerous that way than free. The troops still talked of what had happened in the arena.

Moreover, the man was a lunatic. He'd heard that the orcs had a sky boat, as he'd called it, and said frankly that he'd come here to steal it. Said it as matter of factly as a man would admit eating breakfast.

Such madness, combined with cunning and superlative weapons skills, was something to consider. What would a whole army be like, of men like that? They were bad enough as they were.

And how had he learned about the sky chariot? Presumably from Ahmed's overflights of their camps. But only three days had passed between Ahmed's first raid and the man's capture. Could he have been in the City for some reason, posing as a slave? And for what reason? It was hardly possible. Without speaking orcish, his disguise could hardly have lasted more than a couple of days.

Or did he know orcish?

You could question other men, and their answers, verbal or subverbal, told you what you needed to know. With a little mild torture, screening could be broken. But this man made no useful response unless he wanted to. When his joints were twisted and a hot iron pressed to his cheek, his only reaction was simple awareness.

He would spare him for now. Surely some use could be made of him, some advantage gained, and it might be best if he wasn't damaged.

Though Draco didn't recognize it, he was awed by Nils, was hesitant to torture or damage him further, and would not do so except under stress.

Even if he could make a pact with the tribes of Northmen, Draco reminded himself, the real danger was Ahmed, and only inside the City could he now match the Sudanese. Outside on the open plain the non-psi dog, with his sky chariot and its weapons, would frustrate and defeat any enemy. And the possibility of getting it from him by force or trickery seemed essentially zero.

Meanwhile Ahmed undoubtedly had some plan in motion aimed at forcing a showdown where his advantage would be decisive. Unquestionably that was why he'd used so few bullets on the Northmen; he was saving them to use nearer home. Psi eavesdroppers had reported that operations against the Northmen had been restricted to scattering their herds and stopping their forays onto the plain.

It was irksome to have no knowledge or even hint of what Ahmed planned. Secrets of importance were usually short-lived in the City; this one was remarkably well-kept. And without knowing at least something of it, counter-measures would be difficult to design. In a situation like this, the only defense was to take the offensive.

What he really needed was a sky chariot of his own.

With sudden resolve he got up and strode purposefully from his sanctum to a small chamber on the same floor. There on a table sat the radio of the star people. Beside it sat the officer assigned to monitor broadcasts. The effort had been of no value so far. Only one band could be monitored at a time, so the set was tuned mainly to Band D, which Chandra had used, with occasional brief scans of other bands.

"Out!" snapped Draco. "Wait in the hall."

The man rose to attention, saluted, and closed the heavy door behind him when he left.

"Star ship! Star ship! This is the Lord Draco!"

The answer came promptly in a carefully neutral voice. "This is the star ship *Phaeacia*. Over."

"I want to speak to your captain! At once!"

"Captain Uithoudt is in his quarters. I'll call him."

Draco drummed his fingers on the table, waiting.

"This is Captain Uithoudt. Over."

Draco's voice turned oily, like concentrated sulphuric acid. "Captain, I am sure you recall that I hold certain of your people in my dungeon. I believe you are fond of them. Certainly they are fond of you. They are so far unharmed. Their continued well-being is your responsibility."

He paused for long seconds, letting his words sink in.

"I need your other sky chariot, the one called *Beta*. It should have all the guns you have, and all your . . . ammunition and grenades. You must be careful not to cheat me in this. When I am done with it, you can have it back. I will free your people to return it to you. You will land it tomorrow on a roof of the palace at the same hour as your previous landings. A large red flag will mark the correct roof. Do you have any questions?"

Controlled anger was apparent in the star man's voice. "I can't send *Beta* to you. Without it I can't land to pick people up, or do anything else on the surface."

"If you do not send it, with weapons, you will have no people to pick up."

Again there was a pause, Ram Uithoudt's this time, while Draco enjoyed the man's dilemma. When the answer came, Ram's voice was husky, the words hard and separate like footsteps. "Tomorrow at midday," he said, "I will want to hear the voices of each of my people on this radio so I can know they are all right. I will want to talk with each of them at that time. Otherwise I will send down the *Beta* with weapons more powerful than grenades and automatic rifles, to show you what I can do to you. I'll be listening at midday tomorrow."

The broadcast signal cut abruptly. For seconds Draco sat staring at the set, his face flushed and scowling. Then he got up and strode from the chamber. The fool up there was wasting his bluff; he had no great weapons. And apparently, as he'd suspected, the man didn't even realize his people were held by different factions.

The die was cast. Draco disliked caution. Now he had put things in the hands of fate, and fate almost always smiled at him. The star man would hear the voices of his people, all right. Two of them. He wouldn't talk to them nor they to him, but he would hear their voices, clear and loud. That could be guaranteed. Perhaps afterward the man would be willing to bargain.

Ram sat back in the command seat, face drawn, staring at his knees. What else could he have done?

The orcs respected only power. But what would their response be? He felt in his guts that he'd never see the prisoners again, whether he gave up the *Beta* or not.

Tomorrow morning he'd call Nikko and insist she return to the ship. That would broaden his options. He could change his mind about *Beta* then without stranding her. If he had to lose the others, he at least would not have to leave her behind.

XVII

Svarta fagren, sajflikk henne,
trånt i glumen för d' lunna
Yngling, far t' tvillingarna
på befanningen a Kassi
ty han villa äga jener.

Gryma Kassi, feg erövren,
Belsabubb han åsa hette,
stamfar han a orkahodern.
Imperator, döjd vä kjäären,
klöv ijäl a mäkti Järnhann,
huven ligganne i dyen
hel sväädlent fra blori halsen.

Ålste hon d' mäkti kjämpe,
dråvare a hennes far,
han som stypte jätten Kassi.
Ålste Ynglingen å villa
riska livet, bli d' nödi
a befria ham fra Drekå

[The dark seeress, black-skinned beauty,
yearned to hold again the calm-eyed

128

Youngling, sire of her twin infants
by command of the Lord Kazi
so that he would hold his genes.

Cruel Kazi, cowardly conqueror,
Beelzebub had been his byname,
founder of the orcish armies.
Caesar, rotting by the reed fen,
smote to death by mighty Ironhand,
proud head resting in the muck now,
sword's length from his severed neck lay.

Yes she loved the mighty warrior,
loved the man who'd slain her father,
he who'd felled the ogre Kazi.
Loved the Youngling and was willing
to risk death if that was needed
to deliver him from Draco.]

From—THE JÄRNHANN SAGA,
    Kumalo translation

Moshe the Cerberus was responsible for the security of all prisoners during his watch. Very personally responsible. Should one escape or suicide, Moshe's punishment would be slow, excruciating, and terminal. So he disliked anything not routine and would not tolerate confusion. Confusion made it difficult to monitor thoughts and feelings—nearly impossible to read the subtler nuances.

When the Master was still alive, the danger of escape had been academic, and cerberus—dungeon captain—had been an envied job, comfortable and often enjoyable. While the hazard of prisoner suicide could be minimized by denying means and by monitoring.

During the present power struggle however, two attempts had been made to free men from Draco's dungeon, and rumors of plots were heard almost weekly. Security had been tightened and drills held regularly.

The night watch had been on duty for only minutes when the signal whistle shrilled. It was no alarm, only a signal from the entry guard above, but the two guards at the foot of the stairwell quickly nocked arrows while others clattered out of the guard quarters with pikes or drawn swords.

Moshe stepped to the speaking tube. "What is it?"

"It's the Lady Nephthys, Sir. She wishes to come down with her attendants. She wants to look at the star people and the barbarian."

"Wait twenty breaths, then let them pass."

The Lady Nephthys! The clearest evidence that the Master had favored Lord Draco over the dog Ahmed was his gift to him of Nephthys. Moshe had seen her only at a little distance, but it was said that, close up, her aura was so compelling that statues had lost control of their parts and as punishment had been unmanned with hammer and chisel.

He pulled the lever releasing the entry lock, then strode out of the guard office. Protocol demanded that such a personage be met by the officer in charge. Within the tall stone stairwell he snapped his way through armed men, stopped two paces back from the stone stairs, and stood at attention, a bowman at each side with arrow ready but pointed downward. Behind them were two pairs of swordsmen. Next were four pikemen shoulder to shoulder behind tall shields. Last, just outside the doorway, two men stood by a lever, ready to drop a heavy iron door into place to shut off the stairwell should an attack threaten to succeed.

Three new men, replacing others wounded in an off-duty brawl, had been assigned to standby in the guard room until Moshe could drill them properly.

His stance became more rigid as footsteps sounded softly above; there were no orc boots in her company. Her bodyguards turned into sight—two magnificent blacks, giants, stripped to the waist, armorless except for helmets. Fleetingly beneath his screen, Moshe wondered if they were entire. They must be, he decided, for their muscles were fatless and strongly defined beneath their skin. Entire, then, and well supplied with girls so they could walk tall and haughty, their auras cold and proud despite her nearness.

As soon as she turned into sight behind them, hers was all the aura he was aware of—power, commanding beauty, and a cool sexuality that numbed his will. For seconds he was actually unaware of the presence of her female attendants. As she descended, so gracefully, her visual beauty became one with her aura, and there was no swagger at all to the stiff-spined dungeon captain when he greeted her.

"My Lady!" He couldn't tell whether he'd spoken or only croaked.

Perfect teeth showed briefly, coolly, in her smooth-skinned black face. There was no hair, not even eye-brows, and the shape of her unadorned head was perfect on a strong, regally slim neck. She was slender, rounded, taller than himself, with a filmy white gown caught artfully about her, skin as jet black as her father's. Beside her, her bodyguards were only dark brown, and for the first time in his life Moshe was self-conscious of his own light skin.

It took an effort to maintain his screen so near her. The poor bastards behind him weren't up to it at all, and the wash of flustered awe and fear and male response was a psychic stink. Perhaps behind her cool reserve she laughed.

She spoke, and he led the party from the stairwell, past the rigid standby, to a dully-lit passage between two rows of cells. Some were empty; in others inmates stared or slept. Before the cage of Chandra Queiros she stopped, and slowly he sat up, huddling within his own weak-folded arms. In his unscreened mind, despondency, pain, and dull fear partially gave way to wonder and a vague sexual stirring.

"Ah! The star man," she said. "I hear my Lord had use of him today. I'm told he sings." She examined him deliberately, body and soul, then laughed, a throaty arpeggio in the cell block, and the prisoner, in sudden self-awareness, covered his nakedness with his hands.

"He's a poor thing," she observed as they walked on. "Where is the woman?"

"She has not been returned. Perhaps she's being retained for entertainment." For a moment the orc's mind, unscreened, was outside Nephthys's spell and suddenly sadistically avid.

Dark eyes glanced at him in amusement, and

the cerberus's mind withdrew in confusion behind its screen again.

The barbarian was in the farthest cell.

"Hm-m. So this is the Northman, the one who escaped the arena." She seemed to purr. "Draco won't give him a chance to do that again."

The Northman rose with insolent carelessness, his unscreened mind a meaningless hum discernable among the others only by concentrating. His aura, subdued now and unobtrusive, was none the less one of strength, detachment, purpose.

"He looks different," she commented. "His scalp wasn't shaved then." She turned to one of her bodyguards. "If you faced each other with knives, Mahmut, could you kill him?"

The black face did not change expression, but keen hardness glinted from his mind. Moshe realized then that the man had no tongue, could not speak aloud.

"I'm surprised he seems uninjured," Nephthys continued. "I thought my Lord questioned him."

"Not roughly, my Lady. His face is blistered, as you see, and I'm sure his knees are painful, but that's all."

"No doubt he has plans for him." She examined the prisoner for additional seconds. "I'm disappointed. He isn't as much as I'd heard, close up. There are others as big, and he is only flesh after all. When Draco wishes, he will become quivering flesh."

When the royal party had left, the guardsmen relaxed in their quarters. Alone in the guard room the cerberus took the flagon from his table and drank, but not deeply. That would be unwise on duty. Then he sent it into the guard quarters. As a commander he tried to be generous as well as hard; the combination made for loyalty as well as discipline. When the bottle was returned he swirled what remained, considered briefly, drank again and corked it.

Within an hour the drugged wine had felled all but three—the new men, who'd only feigned drinking. These with swords dispatched the others, walked quickly to the last cell, whispered with their minds to the Northman and took the chains from his ankles. At sword point they led him down the passage. The prisoners who saw felt brief pity, or dread, or nothing, as he passed.

They paused at the guard room long enough to free his wrists, had him don a tunic and black cape, and pulled the hood over his skull, shadowing his face. At the head of the three long flights of stairs, one turned the lock in the entry door and opened it. The guard outside was bored and thinking of other things; he did not expect danger from below, and the telepathic rebels screened well. Although a telepath himself, he was pulled through the door and dead in seconds. One of the three stood in his place to give the others time.

The remaining two walked briskly down the corridor with Nils, in step, orc boots clopping, and soon turned through a plain inset door. Narrow stairs angled sharply upward to a passage whose stone walls were moist with condensation. Occasional oil lamps bracketed on the walls flickered sluggishly in the stale air, and twice they passed man-holes dogged into a wall, each with a massive lock. After some two hundred meters they pulled open a trapdoor and lowered themselves on metal rungs into another passage. Here the air was fouler, the lamps so low and far apart it was like night. His guides took off their boots, slung them over their shoulders, and led him quietly through the darkness. At length they climbed upward into an unlit room, redonned their boots, and exited beneath stars. Alert for the sound or sense of a possible soft-shod night patrol, they entered a nearby alley. One straddled a man-hole, gripped the stone cover by a ring with both hands, and removed it with a grunt. He lowered himself and disappeared.

"Now you," the other whispered to Nils. "I must stay up here to replace the cover."

Nils lowered himself, hung by his fingers for a second, then dropped into blackness. His tortured knees buckled at the bottom, sprawling him onto rough stone paving. Carefully he rose, and heard the manhole cover being lowered into place.

His remaining escort whispered to him in Anglic. "I'm taking you to a storm sewer that you can follow to the canal. They have gratings across them at intervals that a man can't crawl through; this joins one of them below the last grate. If half that is said of you is true, once you cross the canal you should be able to get away without any trouble."

Psychically Nils nodded. The man was barefoot again, and they padded through the narrow tunnel in utter darkness, his guide with a sense of knowing the way. Before long they came to an end, a door, and the Northman sensed the other feeling for a latch, finding it. It would not move. He grasped it with both hands, still couldn't budge it, and fear surged through him. Nils nudged him aside, explored with his fingers, closed powerful fists on it and pulled, then jerked. Then he pushed, finally lunging against it with a heavy shoulder. The orc took out his sword and pried, carefully at first, then desperately so that the point snapped.

His fear dulled to despondency. "We're trapped," he said with his mind. "This route's been blocked. And we can't get back out the way we came; it's too high."

Nils's mind questioned.

"No, the other way is a dead end just beyond the shaft we came down."

Reaching up, Nils found he could touch the overhead. "Let's go back to the shaft," he thought. "There's something I want to try."

Mentally the man shrugged. Nils led, one hand following the wall, the fingers of the other brushing along the overhead until they found the emptiness of the shaft down which they'd dropped. It was perhaps a meter and a half wide, and round, impossible to climb. He dropped to one knee, hands against the damp wall. "Squat on my shoulders," he instructed. "When I get up, put your hands on the side of the shaft and stand. See if you can reach the cover."

Slowly Nils stood with his burden, and carefully the orc rose to his feet; with the return of hope had come fear again.

"I can't reach it."

"Stand on my hands and I'll lift you."

The man raised his left foot, put it on one of Nils's palms, then repeated with the other, steadying himself shakily with his hands against the wall. Nils grasped both feet firmly, and slowly raised him to arm's length overhead. He sensed the orc reaching upward almost hesitantly, touching pavement above, fingers feeling for the edges that defined the cover, finding them. Nils braced his legs, the thick muscles of his arms and shoulders swelling as the man pushed upward against the heavy disk. It gave a little, a centimeter, then the man's arms were fully extended and could lift no higher. Nils raised up slowly on the balls of his feet, and for just a moment they gained a little more. Then the orc fell backward, striking his head against the side of the shaft before landing heavily on the stones below. There was a stab of pain in his left elbow.

Nils knelt beside him. The orc radiated hopelessness. "I couldn't raise it," he whispered. "Not enough. It must be eight centimeters thick."

Nils's mind acknowledged. "Now what?" he asked.

"We stay here until they come for us."

"Come for us?"

"They have dogs. For tracking, a dog's nose is better than telepathy. When they find what happened in the dungeon they'll track us down."

Nils sensed the man fumbling through a belt pouch, hunting for death. He pressed an object like a pebble into Nils's palm. "Swallow it," he instructed. "You'll go to sleep and there will be no wakening. If they take us alive, after what happened. . . . When they have done with us, even dying would bring no peace. The agony would follow beyond death itself."

Nils regarded him calmly, and after a moment the other mind shrugged. The man put the pill in his dry mouth, far back on his tongue, swallowed, shuddered, then breathed deeply and relaxed. Nils sat beside him. Presently the orc slumped against him and Nils cradled his head and shoulders. The mind was drifting, fading, the breathing shallow. Before long Nils was alone.

XVIII

Orcs still filed into the arena, into sections reserved for each legion, subsections for each cohort. The sunny side was empty; there were now no horse barbarians to fill it. After the battle of the burning prairie and the death of Kazi, almost a year earlier and so far away, their hordes had deserted the orcs. They'd careened into central Europe a disorganized mob, been decisively beaten by the united Germanic knights, and broken into scores of marauding bands. So said the reports.

There were more Asian tribes, thought Kamal the Grim, eastward on the desert steppes and plateaus and barren mountains, but there was no longer a Kazi to gather them. He turned and scanned the shady side, which in summer was the orc side. Even here many upper rows would be empty, reflecting the bleaching bones scattered in the northern Ukraine.

The command box was already filled, with chiefs of cohorts and legions circulating, conversing, shadowed by their bodyguards. They'd associated freely while the Master still lived, when future and con-

quest had seemed assured and factionalism remained embryonic. Some had served together in
old campaigns. Now those of opposing factions
saw one another almost only at the games. At any
other time it would suggest dangerous disloyalty
to their consul.

The situation aggravated Kamal. Reduced as they
were, and without allies, they were still easily the
strongest military force in the known world. They'd
suffered a defeat, a severe setback, but they still
had the power to conquer. Their present ineffec-
tiveness, he told himself, was their own doing.
Paralyzed by factionalism, they couldn't even sally
out in force to scatter the Northmen on their
fringe. For that required, if not union, at least the
forbearance of one faction while the other did
the job.

And that wouldn't happen without the victory of
one faction or the other. They all knew it. But
most wanted their own faction to win; for command officers there was mortal danger in defeat.
And for those inclined to risk conspiracy, spies and
other telepaths made it too dangerous.

Union would come eventually though, and when
it did, orc power would be felt again. Europe would
fall.

Once more he scanned the stands. It might be
better, Kamal thought, if we didn't hold games for
awhile. A stadium two-thirds empty reminded the
men of their reduction in strength. Few realized
the abstract—that their force was still great, their
potential overwhelming. They knew only what their
eyes and memories told them: a year earlier they
had been one great army which, with its allies,

filled these stands. And the games had been presided over by the Master, all-powerful, feared, adored, and he'd been called the Undying. Now they looked across at empty seats, and were presided over by himself—a soldier, not a god. His role as master of the games was a demonstration of weakness, a symptom of division. The lowest soldier knew that Kamal the Grim was the only high-ranking officer trusted by both consuls.

Draco swaggered over to him and clapped his shoulder. "How stands it with the Games Master? I seldom see you anymore, Kamal."

"That's no fault of mine," Kamal answered sourly.

Draco's eyebrows rose. "No fault of yours? I think it is." He lowered his voice as if half the men in the command box were not telepaths. "If you changed allegiance we could see a lot of each other. I appreciate a good man and a real orc. As it stands, you command a legion but have no seat in the council of your commander. With me it would be different.

"By the way, I don't see our friend Ahmed here. Is he sick? Surely every orc is here unless duty forbids, or mortal illness."

Kamal's expression was grumpy. "I'm a soldier, not a power seeker or politician. I have no wish to sit on any man's council. I'll let others decide what should be done, as long as they give me a share in the doing."

Draco's mouth smiled. Kamal, he thought, you non-psi dog, you screen as well as most telepaths but you're a poor liar. Your only guile is silence. I not only know *how* you think, old comrade, but often *what* you think, without needing to read you.

"No wish for influence? I can't believe that. You

haven't fully considered your answer. You have a sense of right and wrong. You know the plans the Master had and what he held to be important. This, for instance." Draco gestured about at the stadium. "He had it built while the army still lived in tents. It had priority over dwellings; only the palace preceded it. Before either of us was born, he presided here. The games and entertainments are to demonstrate our superiority, and in his time, attendance was compulsory. Now that the Master is dead, your dear Ahmed is above the law and doesn't trouble to come. Not surprising perhaps—his father was a slave, not an orc, and he grew up in the comfort of his father's apartment, not an orcling pen. How can you stomach a man like that?"

"I have no complaint with him. He is a strong and able leader, and he gave me my legion."

"Hah! You led the Imperial Guard cohort, the elite of the army! Are you sure it was you Ahmed wanted? Or did he want your cohort, promoting you to gain them? With me you'd have influence along with rank. I have real orcs for counselors, too, not a fat eunuch slave like that damned Yusuf. And *I* haven't abandoned the Master's dreams and plans."

"The Master himself had slaves as counselors; Ahmed's father was one of them."

"*The Master was the Master! There is no comparison!*" Draco almost hissed now with intensity. "Listen, old comrade, I know the kind of orc you are, and I hate to see you back a swine like that. I knew you when we were boys together. And when we were centurions in the same cohort I saw the kind of man you'd grown to be, the kind of leader you were becoming. A real orc, but not a common orc. An orc with high intelligence and a sense of destiny, providing his own discipline, thinking beyond the next orgy.

"You *should* sit in the councils of power. Don't let go the Master's dreams and give yourself to the ambitions of a slave's son who abandoned the Master as soon as he was dead."

Kamal answered coldly. "Perhaps I know Ahmed better than you do. His heart is an orc's even if his stomach isn't, and his brain is an orc's. He is as loyal to the Master as anyone is."

Draco's eyes narrowed. "Are you sure? Who did the Master entrust the empire to when he went to war, and who was it he took along to keep his eye on? Think about it.

"And which of us did he plan to make his chief lieutenant? Who did he give Nephthys to?" His voice softened, his words slowed. "Now there was a gift. You can't imagine. She is like a banquet, and the others are dry bread. When she touches me . . ." His shiver seemed involuntary.

"It's too bad I don't have others like her, to reward my chief lieutenants with. Sometimes I wonder if I should share her. It was to me she was given of course, and a gift like that should not be used carelessly. But on the other hand I am the consul, and a man of great power. I can take or give as I see fit."

Kamal said nothing, and his face remained sober, but when he stood at the railing to begin the ceremonies he was licking dry lips.

Yes, old comrade, Draco thought behind his screen, I know you well. I know your strengths *and*

I remember your weaknesses. You and your legion are as valuable as a pinnace, if used correctly, and I believe you'll be mine. You're no fool; you saw through my words. But you won't be able to forget them.

XIX

But the Philistines took him, and put out his eyes, and brought him down to Gaza; and bound him with fetters of brass . . .

HOLY BIBLE, Judges 16:22.

Three kilometers below, the nightbound prairie registered mostly featureless gray to the infrared scanner. Darker patches were marshes, with the black lines of creeks here and there. A half-dozen night flights and several sessions with the two starmen had made the pilot a fair novice infrared interpreter, and the consul relied on him.

Ahmed stared morosely without seeing. Capture of the pinnace had seemed an important victory. Certainly it had involved a major risk. But he'd been unable to take real advantage of it. Or perhaps unwilling to, he thought. When a man has a resource like the pinnace he may become too cautious, afraid to risk, hesitant to make the next move.

Major decisions usually were difficult for him, and he preferred to delay them. He could always see a score of possible disasters waiting. Draco was different; he jumped to decisions. To a disgusting degree the man ignored possible side effects, complications, uncertainties. That was his major strength and major weakness.

It was less comfortable to sense countless unknowns, to try logically and objectively to balance a score of unpredictables, staring fruitlessly at a half-seen web leading to various possible results, many of which were intolerable. And when he could delay no longer, Ahmed recognized, too often he had to ignore the complications anyway and, like Draco, act regardless.

The plan he'd decided on was more dangerous than any he'd seriously considered before. It could well abort, of course, and nothing would be lost but time. The odds were strong that the Northmen wouldn't agree. Perhaps it had been a subtle way of postponing longer, for if they refused, he'd have to come up with something else—a new plan, another perhaps slow decision.

But if they did agree—if they did—a course of action would begin that would end either in quick victory or utter defeat. The numerous small dangers of indefinite maneuver would be replaced by the stark danger of an early showdown. Success would depend on timing, secrecy, and more than anything else on the reaction of his legions.

He hoped the Northmen would agree. It occurred to him that something inside him might be seeking a quick end instead of a quick victory, release instead of success.

His always stiff spine became fractionally stiffer. When he finally decided, he did not hesitate to act.

And his decisions, if slow, were none the less likely to be bold, unpredictable by a clod like Draco.

The gray on the viewscreen darkened, marking the canopy of a forest rooted below drought and rich in cellular water, its irregular upper level and countless billions of needles an intense complexity of evaporating-radiating surfaces. A lighter strip marked an open valley in their line of flight.

The pilot zoomed the viewer, and in seconds found the men they were to meet, a cluster of white dots in the grayness. They were waiting a little distance from their small signal fire, away from its small light. It would be good, he thought, to swoop down and chop them to pieces in the darkness; what a surprise that would give them.

Instead he raised the commast and started settling earthward.

Nikko sensed the quickening of the chiefs and the men who waited with them. It was a slight straightening of backs, a movement of heads, an awareness and heightened readiness that required no psi to sense. But when she strained her ears and peered upward she saw nothing.

And then it was there, fifty meters from them, settling to the ground, a blacker darkness in the moonless night. They got up quietly and started toward it, spreading out a little in caution. She followed close behind until they formed an open semicircle not far outside the force shield.

The voice from the commast was quiet in the waiting night, speaking Anglic. Its softness surprised Nikko.

"I am Ahmed, consul of the orcs. I have an offer to make you, one you will find hard to refuse."

Sten Vannaren translated for the gathering—primarily the Council of Chiefs and the War Council, which in part were the same men. His reply was terse: "Tell us your offer."

"I rule a strong army, half of all the Northern orcs. My enemy, Draco, rules the other half. Soon he and I will war with one another, and I want your help. He hates Northmen. If he defeats me, he will march against you and destroy you."

When Sten finished the translation, old Axel Stornäve spoke. His words were dry and bored, and Sten put the same quality into his Anglic. "Orcs have marched on us before, and many did not live to regret it. Why should we be concerned if they march again?"

"When we fought before," Ahmed replied, "you were only an army of warriors. You could move freely, and we didn't succeed in trapping you, although we came close. Now you have your women and children with you, and many others who aren't warriors, whom you must protect. And you must protect your cattle or starve.

"And if Draco defeats me he'll have the sky chariot to attack you with. Unfortunately it will be of little use to me against him if he keeps the fighting within the City. As he knows."

This time it was the deep growl of Kniv Listi that Sten translated. "If orcs fight orcs until one side wins, there will be many dead orcs. We don't object to that. And after you have butchered one another, how will you destroy us?"

"You don't appreciate our numbers," Ahmed replied. "Only one of our armies was in the Ukraine. Our soldiers are as numerous as all your people together, including your women and infants. And if Draco wins, there will be the sky chariot. Also, we know now how you fight, the kind of tactics you use. If Draco makes war against you, he will not be ignorant and careless as we were at first in the Ukraine.

"And finally, though Draco and I hate each other, our men do not. Before our losses become great, one side will win a clear advantage. When that happens, the soldiers of the weaker side will throw down their leader and acknowledge the rule of the other.

"But if you ally yourself with me, I will surely win, for although you are not numerous, you are skilled and savage fighters. And if you help me, I will reward you. When I have won, I'll take my army away and leave this country to you. Our empire is very large, and much of it lies south of the Black Sea and the Great Sea. For a long time our soldiers have grumbled at the winters here, and for me, I do not love this land."

The chiefs drew back a bit, dim in the darkness, talking quietly, Nikko listening at the fringe. After a bit Sten spoke again to the orc. "To fight at your city we first have to get there across the Great Meadow. How do you propose we do that without being trapped in the open?"

"Since I have the sky chariot, Draco dares not send out patrols, even at night. The sky chariot can see in the darkness. So he probably will not know you are coming. If his spies find out, and he is foolish enough to go out to attack you, I can scatter his legions with fear and death. My sky chariot will be your protection until you get there. Then, of course, you'll have to fight."

"You say you'll protect us on the Great Meadow.

How can we know you won't attack us instead? How can we know it isn't a trap you offer instead of a country?"

There was a short lapse before Ahmed answered. "I have left my mind perfectly open as I talked with you. Have you no telepaths?"

There followed quiet conversation among the Northmen. Three of their newly trained telepaths were there. "We can't read their thoughts," one said, "because they think in orcish. But we can read mood and feeling, which are more reliable if less explicit. The one who spoke is ruthless and unpredictable. At present he intends to keep his word, but he is not a man to trust. All three of us read it the same."

After a few moments of thought, Kniv Listi spoke, full-voiced, with Sten translating. "Our telepaths tell us you mean what you say. But once you have won, you will command all the orcs, and we will be far from our forests. You will have no more need of allies then, heavily out-numbered allies who could be attacked from the sky. What proof can you give that you won't change your mind and turn on us?"

While the two Northmen spoke in turns, Scandinavian, then Anglic, Nikko felt herself filling with impulse, excitement, determination. As quickly as they were done she called out loudly and clearly. "Ahmed! Will you give up your hostages as a sign of good will? If you turn them over to these people, perhaps they might trust you."

She felt unseen eyes around her while Sten translated for the Northmen.

"The hostages are star people," the consul answered coldly, "and mean nothing to the Northmen.

You are a hostage yourself, and a fool, not a chief. Beware of talking out of turn. They are indulgent with you but their patience is not limitless."

She felt small and alone, intimidated, among the tall grim chiefs who scowled at her in the darkness.

"Not all your hostages are star people," she answered. "You have Nils Järnhann in your prison, the Northman giant who escaped from your arena once."

Sten abandoned protocol. "They have Nils? How do you know?"

"Ilse told me," she replied. "Now that I'm a hostage you don't let me use the radio anymore. But just after you left for this meeting, the signal started buzzing, and I showed Hild how to turn it on. It was Ilse, and you weren't there, so she asked to talk to me. She'd had a vision of Nils held captive by the orcs. And it wasn't a premonition; they have him *now*. She wanted you to know."

She stood shivering while Sten translated for the Northmen and Kniv questioned the telepaths. They agreed she had not lied. The chiefs were utterly intent now as Sten spoke for Kniv Listi.

"Why didn't you tell us you hold our Yngling prisoner?"

For long seconds the orc did not answer. "I don't hold him prisoner," he said at last.

Kniv questioned the telepaths again. "He speaks the truth," one said. "We are agreed. But he doesn't tell all he knows."

"What else then?" Sten demanded for the war leader. "Have you killed him?"

"I have never had him prisoner and I have not killed him."

"Then perhaps your enemy holds him!"

Ahmed didn't answer. "You struck deep with that one," the telepaths told Kniv. "His enemy does hold the Yngling."

Listi scowled thoughtfully. "Nils Järnhann can do what other men can't," he said to Sten. "While he lives there is hope for him. But if we war against the orc that holds him, he won't live long. Tell this Ahmed if he can return our Yngling to us alive and whole, *then* we will talk about alliance. Otherwise we will let the orcs kill each other."

"Sten, wait!" Nikko broke in. She spoke his language now. "There is more about Nils! Ilse saw more than I told you!" She listened in fright to her own words tumbling out, afraid of what she was saying, afraid she was making a terrible mistake in telling it here and now. "Sten, Ilse saw them . . . she told me she saw them . . . *pierce his eyes! Nils is blind, Sten! Nils is blind!*"

Ahmed stood tensely, staring through the transparent hull at the indistinct group in the darkness.

"Whatever the star woman told them that time," Yusuf said quietly, "it made them very angry. Not at her, but very angry."

Listening to them, Ahmed didn't need telepathy to know they were angry. Grim and angry. At last the one who spoke Anglic addressed him with a deadly voice.

"We will fight your enemy. He has *put out the eyes* of our Yngling. We will ride from here at the second dawning. You will tell us how to know your soldiers from the others so we do not kill them by mistake. And when your enemy is captured, he is ours to settle with. *Ours.* Do not forget that. *Be very careful that you do not forget that.*"

Alpha sledded swiftly through the night sky.

"Indeed, my Lord, I was surprised at their rage," Yusuf was saying. "I'd read them as a hardheaded people, men with control of their passions, or indeed with little that we ordinarily think of as passion at all. I tell you frankly, I never expected that they would agree to your offer. That act of Draco's cut some very deep taboo."

Ahmed's mood swelled with grim pleasure. "They've shown a weakness. I see them differently now. Perhaps when it is over we will stay after all. At any rate the die is cast."

Yusuf withdrew into contemplation and they rode briefly in silence. "My Lord," he said finally, "let me offer unasked advice. Be careful of the Northmen. When the star woman told them what had been done to their hero, their anger was not ordinary rage that destroys wit and logic, however reckless their decision seems. There was a terribly deadly intention; they reeked of danger. They felt like the storm from the steppe that sucks up men and horses and spits out broken rags."

Ahmed pursed his lips in the darkness. "You are always somber, my friend, but now you dramatize. That's not like you. The Northmen are nothing to trifle with, I grant you. That's why even their small numbers will make the difference and assure us victory. But angry men, vengeful men, make mistakes."

Yusf stared gloomily into the night as if watching something. "It wasn't hot anger to thicken the wits. Their rage was cold, with an edge like a razor."

Now Ahmed brooded also. After all, Yusuf was psychic, and there were many dangers. What whisper might he hear from the future?

The barbarians had grinned in battle—laughed and crowed aloud and fought with the strength and vigor of the possessed. And they always won. Now perhaps they *were* possessed. Goose flesh rose on his arms and crawled across his scalp. He wondered if they'd grin in the battle to come, and what their laughter might then be like.

Yusuf was right. He would take no liberties.

XX

Her world was bright and clear and detailed. Her senses were more than sight and hearing, more than touch, taste, heat and smell, more than awareness of orientation and gravitic vectors—the usual data sources. With her, even the ordinary senses were more sensitive, more aware.

Her mind lacked some of the usual barriers; she was less constrained by past pain and hurtful emotions, more open to data at variance with general beliefs.

Hers was a world of discovery and growth. Possibilities became accessible to her.

Her eyes had closed; she felt no need for visual input just then. The fetus moved within her body, shifting uncomfortably in the cramped quarters, found a new position and became quiet again. She was aware of it but gave it no attention.

She did not grieve at the blinding of Nils, although at first the knowledge had shocked her. And she did not worry over what might happen next, although she was by no means indifferent. Simply, she would see what she could do. Now her attention focused on a question and remained there, examining.

Celia Uithoudt knocked lightly on the cabin door, waited, then knocked again.

"Ilse?"

Her waiting reflected uncertainty. By now the whole crew knew what the young Earth woman had reported to the surface. After a moment Celia turned the knob and looked in. Ilse sat on a small folded rug, her straight back to the door. Celia's eyes rested on her briefly. Softly she closed the door again and went down the corridor to the dispensary.

As a safety margin the *Phaeacia* carried two physicians. So far they'd had little to do. She leaned back in the dispensary reading chair, punched in the novel she'd begun, and relaxed. For a while she read quietly with only the small movements normal to sitting, but before long became restless. Finally she put the tape on hold and turned to scan the room. She was alone.

She got up, stepped hesitantly to the door of the small laboratory-pharmacy and peered in, then looked into surgery. No one. Shaking her head she went back to the chair and began reading again.

The possibility had occurred to Ilse and she'd tried it. It turned out not to be difficult for her. She'd done something a bit like it before, in healing, when she would focus her attention on the sick or injured part and concentrate on its wholeness and normal functioning. In this case she'd focused on Celia, concentrating on being beside her. Suddenly she'd been there, surrounded by white enamel and stainless steel, next to the woman who'd become her friend.

She'd been surprised when Celia sensed her presence. Although the woman had shown no sign of being even a latent telepath, she had sensed the psychic presence.

Then Ilse was back in her own cabin, in her still erectly seated body. It had remained upright, the heartbeat slow and regular. But it seemed to her that, without her attendance, the body might not long survive.

And Celia had felt her, although she had not known what it was she felt. So presumably would almost anyone except the totally psi-deaf. Apparently the psyche was sensed more strongly when away from the body.

Again she put herself in the dispensary with her friend. Celia's mind was composed, absorbing the lines of print. Gradually Ilse impinged more strongly, until the mind beside her showed hints of disturbance. The eyes did not scan as rhythmically. A grain of unease irritated the mind, which tried to shut out the irritation.

Ilse withdrew again to her body and examined results. She could enter the space of a non-psi and be noticed or not noticed at will, according to impingement, intention. But could she enter the presence of telepaths and be unnoticed? Or be noticed selectively, by one and not another? Nils would probably be guarded by a telepath.

Ram was the only telepath on board besides herself, a fitful and very limited one who could provide only a limited test. Subconsciously he still tended strongly to reject what his talent picked up.

Carefully, lightly, she focused on him. He sat in his command chair, glancing back and forth from computer screen to keyboard as his index finger moved deliberately, punching out questions from a checklist. His mind was restless, only a trivial part of it occupied by the routine task. It reflected a sense of futility, and the tinge of paranoia she had noticed.

His unconscious awareness of her was so vague that she recognized it only because she was looking for it. It was not an awareness of another being in his space, but simply of something not quite right, warily ignored.

She withdrew to her body again, for a few moments monitoring its functioning, then focused her attention away again, this time on a place. The tent was gone, and she was on its site, in a circle of yellowed grass around a bull's eye of wood ashes. Tiny huts hunkered around her, low and drab in the long rays of evening sunlight. There were no voices or any trace of human minds.

She hadn't tried to move about disembodied before in any way analogous to walking. She found now that she could, and looked into a nearby hut. It was stripped, as she knew it would be.

She conjoined again, instantaneously but softly, raised her body from the rug and drank at the washbowl. So she could project to a distance, to either familiar people or familiar places, and "move around" while there, but she did not feel safe to stay away from the body too long.

She needed experience, she decided, and to test herself against competent psis. Perhaps Hannes was still alive; she hadn't heard of her brother since the battle at Doppeltanne, a thousand miles and eight months ago. He was an excellent telepath, as sensitive as almost anyone, and no harm would be done if he discovered her.

XXI

It was dangerous, but not nearly as dangerous as the alternatives. And if it worked—if it worked he'd have a double victory, over Ahmed and over the Northmen.

The greatest danger was now. Draco ground his teeth unconsciously. Where *was* the gloomy fool? The consul's irritable jumpiness did not lessen the intentness with which he monitored. To be caught here on Ahmed's territory . . . A centurion's helmet and breast plate made a thin disguise for a well-known man, even at dusk. And he couldn't be sure the note had gone through unintercepted. Carried in the mouth it was safer than a spoken message, if the bearer didn't know what was written on it and remembered to swallow if stopped. But if the swallowing was seen and interpreted, a slit gullet would quickly give it up.

More sets of orc boots approached the alley mouth, but this time it was Kamal who strode past, accompanied by his psi-aid and one other. A quick thought flicked, and when Kamal was a dozen meters farther on, Draco and his companion fell in behind them. Two hundred meters farther and

Kamal turned, strode up a low flight of entry stairs, and entered a building. Draco followed.

Kamal was waiting just inside. Otherwise the hallway was deserted, but Draco sensed frightened awareness behind thin wooden doors, a listening to the sound of iron heel plates. Slaves were slaves, whether like these they had status and an apartment or were common drudges crouching in a slave barracks. He spit. They lived powerless and in fear—bloodless, breath-in-throat, honorless fear.

Kamal paused at a door, shoved it open and strode in. Those inside had interpreted the sounds and pauses, and stood waiting. The man was middle-aged, the woman young. They exuded propitiation and submission toward their user-protector. The man hesitated, then bobbed his head and disappeared through an inner door while the woman remained.

Draco grinned. Old Kamal! She was a beauty, and certainly never showed herself in the streets. A dancer, by her looks, who probably performed for her neighbors. One of them had no doubt reported her beauty and grace to Kamal in hope of some reward.

She was undoubtedly an exceptional lay, with something of a hold on the hard-bitten legionary, if he let her stay here with her husband instead of taking her into his harem. Or perhaps he found pleasure in humiliating the man by using her here in his presence.

Yes, she was a good one. It showed less in her aura than in Kamal's irritation now in having business to transact instead of pleasure. But it was a good place for it.

"Get out," Kamal said drily to her. "We want to talk."

She stood confused.

"Take her out of here," he snapped at his orderly. "And I don't want them listening at the door."

The man nodded, gripped her arm and led her to the door through which her husband had passed.

"And Dmitri! Do not molest her! Remember who she belongs to."

The soldier turned, saluted, and closed the door behind him.

Kamal looked at Draco and spoke in an undertone. "This had better be important. Meeting you secretly like this could mean my bones."

The consul smirked, and kept his voice low too. "It's important, all right. But first, before I forget, Nephthys instructed me to give you her warmest greeting. I can't, of course. She hopes you'll be our guest soon." He turned and clapped the shoulder of the soldier who'd accompanied him. "And now, Artos, I want you to tell my friend what you've learned."

Artos was small for an orc, but sinewy and shrewd-looking. "As a centurion in the Second Legion," he began, "I was known as one of the most sensitive telepaths in the army. So when this happened—" he held out a wrist with no hand—"my Lord Draco made me the monitor of his psi tuner.

"I came to have a feeling for the tuner, a feeling I can't describe. So with my Lord's permission I removed the crystal from it. I'm not free to say what experiments were made or what I did, but the crystal has been recut and reground so that my mind is now in resonance with it."

Draco interrupted. "It no longer looks like an

esper crystal." He grinned widely. "It's just another stone in a jewelled goblet now, in Ahmed's wine pantry. It's been there for weeks, and in his room several times, but until last night it told us nothing worth knowing." He nudged the maimed telepath with his mind. "Tell us what you read last night, and keep your voice down."

The man nodded. "It was about midnight," he murmured. "Ahmed had wine and a girl brought to him. He was preoccupied, and finished with her rather quickly, but the goblet stayed while he sat and thought.

"He'd been away in his sky chariot. He'd used his, um, radio, you see, to talk to the Northmen. They have a star woman hostage, the Northmen, and her radio; the star people are total cretins. And Ahmed knew about the radio.

"So after dark he'd flown to a meeting he'd set up with the Northmen scum, and sitting safe in his chariot he made an agreement with them. They are to send their army here and Ahmed promised to use his sky chariot to protect them from attack in the open, in case my Lord learned of their approach. When they reached the City, they're to join with Ahmed's legions to attack us.

"And he promised that when he's the master he'll take the army away to Egypt and leave this country to the Northmen. The City of Kazi a barbarian sty! That's to be their reward. And it's uncanny, but he really means to do it, give the country to them!"

"Garbage!" Kamal snorted, then lowered his voice. "I know him better than that. Your story's a fable." But as he said it he turned questioningly to his psi aid. It was almost too preposterous to be a lie.

The aid looked at him squarely. "The man left his mind wide open to me while he told it," he answered flatly. "He told truthfully what he read in Ahmed's mind, altering nothing and holding nothing back. There is no question about it."

Kamal scowled thoughtfully for a time. "What is it you want me to do?" he asked at last, and his voice was as hard as his eyes.

"Take Ahmed prisoner for me. Trusted as you are, you can move the men you need close to his apartment. I'll leave it to your imagination to figure out how; you know the situation much better than I."

Kamal's flinty eyes fixed on the consul's and he made no answer.

"All right," Draco spat out, "kill him then, if you think he'd be too dangerous as a prisoner. Then announce his crime—treason against the Master—declare yourself commander of his troops, and join me against the Northmen."

The legionary continued to stare wordlessly at Draco, his eyes glittering now.

"She remains mine," Draco growled at the unspoken demand, "but you will be our guest from time to time."

For a moment Kamal still stood motionless, then nodded and drew his sword.

"Dmitri!"

The door opened quickly at his call.

"Kill them in there," he murmured. "I must be sure there is no leak."

The orc turned, pulling at his hilt. There were no screams, but they heard the husband grunt, and the woman whimpered briefly. When the orderly reappeared he was wiping his sword on a piece of her gown. As soon as he'd sheathed it, Kamal cut him down.

"No leaks," he said meaningfully.

The one-handed Artos darted for the door but Draco was on him, thrusting with his short sword. "No leaks," Draco husked. "What about him?" He nodded toward Kamal's psi aid.

Kamal shook his head. "He's as close to me as my own breath. Whoever kills him answers to me."

Draco's response was inward and screened. *Already you grow insolent, old friend. I'll kill him myself when the time comes, and you'll watch. Then I'll kill you.*

The audience chamber of Timur Karim Kazi had been unused since he'd left to conquer Europe. It was small—six meters square and four high—with walls of glossy obsidian and carpeted with thick black furs so cleverly joined they looked like a single huge pelt. There was only one seat, the throne on its dais, but pillows lay around the other three walls. Tall narrow windows let in light.

So he's using the Master's audience chamber already, Kamal thought. That arrogant filth. If he sits on the Master's throne I'll kill him here and now.

Draco, sensing his anger and suspecting its cause, did not approach the high seat.

"I'm told you did the job with your own hand and he gave you no trouble," he said. "I appreciate the gift of Yusuf. I prevailed on him to tell everything he knew. I never imagined the Turk could be so talkative, so co-operative. The Northmen should

be leaving their mountains at daybreak. I'll observe them from the pinnace, which they think of
as their protection. The young men who flew it for
Ahmed are happy to fly it for me.

"I'm appointing you field commander and leave
the final say on tactics to your judgment. I suggest though that you plan to meet the Northmen
at least two day's ride from here."

Kamal nodded. "Four or five days from now,
depending on how fast they travel. I'll let them
ride into a sack and pull the drawstring on them
in the morning to have as many hours of daylight
as possible. Otherwise some of them might lose
themselves in the darkness and escape. It should
be easy to time it, with you sitting in the sky
keeping track of them. I suggest you attack them
before I do, from the air, as soon as they're aware
of us. That should disorganize them and we'll chop
them to pieces with minimum losses of our own."

Draco smiled and held out his hand. "It sounds
beautiful—more like slaughter than battle."

*And when it's over, old comrade, I'll drop down
and pick you up—to take you where none of your
men are at hand. You're too dangerous—and too
powerful now, and possibly ambitious after all. You'll
give me the pleasure you denied me from Ahmed.*

"And Kamal," Draco said, "when the Northmen
are destroyed, I want you to spend some time with
me in harem. Someone there is hungry to see you."

XXII

Nils lay motionless on the stone ledge that was his cot. Because of his wounds, straw had been piled on it and he had a coarse woolen blanket to crawl under. Draco was saving him for something.

For four days he'd lain quietly, rousing only for food and water. He had thirsted often. But mostly he'd been in a trance-like state, his mind focused quietly on healing nerves and outraged tissues. During the last few hours, however, he'd been doing something else.

It was fortunate that the dungeon captain was a psi. Otherwise there'd be no chance at all.

The dungeon captain sat in the guard room at the end of the cell block, monitoring subconsciously while he thought of other things. Occasionally he brought his attention to it, sorting among the emanations of the prisoners, sifting their thoughts, moods and emotions through his critical mind.

Nils's awareness had entered it too, but undetected, formless, a slight and undefined watchfulness no more than vague smoke at twilight. He could afford no misstep. If the orc discovered what he was doing, there would be no second chance.

He assumed the orc didn't know of the technique and wouldn't be on guard against it. Even Raadgiver, shrewd old psi of the Inner Circle, apparently hadn't known of it. It was Ilse who'd discovered it, used it to murder Zühtü Hakki and escape the horse barbarians.

Carefully, patiently, he followed the orc's thoughts, feeling their tone, their hue, absorbing the essence of the man.

Sometimes Yitzhak focused on a specific mind; he could discern details and sense subtleties better that way. Now he turned his attention to the Northman. The aura was subdued, less powerful, but essentially unchanged. Usually a man's aura deteriorated utterly when he'd been maimed, and blinding was one of the most devastating maimings. When someone was blinded, locked in a dungeon, and facing certain torture without hope of escape, his aura was the aura of death.

Beneath the Northman's aura was only a soft and meaningless psionic hum. Thoughtfully Yitzhak scratched his cheek, unaware that the impulse was not his own.

His attention shifted to the star man. Until today the mind had been a study in raw sensitivity. Usually it was difficult to keep someone so responsive for long; they became comatose. This one, however, they had returned to delicious rawness repeatedly, by abusing his woman. Then, during Khalil's watch, he'd been taken away for an hour or so. He'd been returned with his mind deeply collapsed, although they hadn't used him very roughly. It even seemed he might actually die without serious physical injury.

Something touched Nils's consciousness softly,

and softly he withdrew from the mind of the orc. It had not been a thought; almost it had been nothing at all. A presence, the faintest presence of Ilse. He knew she wasn't there physically, and grasped intuitively what she had done. She strengthened, and through her he saw himself a supine body beneath the coarse gray wool. A touch from his mind warned her and she drew back to the edge of thereness. Anything either of them transmitted—thoughts, pictures—might be picked up by the dungeon captain. Jerkily Nils transmitted then, gusts of Scandinavian as in a troubled dream, still picturing himself on the sleeping ledge, the image wavering, collapsing.

So the eyeless barbarian dreamed. Yitzhak viewed briefly until the mind settled back into its even and featureless hum. It would be interesting to know what Draco had in mind for that one. The patrol commander who'd found him had made a serious mistake, putting out his eyes. It was commonplace to blind a fugitive slave out of hand. Blind him or her and let the creature wander sightless about the streets, pushed, dragged, worked over with knife tips, fists, whatever orc ingenuity and humor came up with until they died of shock, pain and exhaustion.

But only a fool would blind a personal prisoner of the consul.

He'd stop at the Square after watch, Yitzhak decided, and see if the stupid bastard was still alive. Maybe there'd be enough consciousness left to be worth watching. Probably not though. The common soldiers generally got carried away and lost whatever finesse they had when given a patrol commander to play with.

(Yitzhak got up and sauntered into one of the cell-block lanes. A man needed to move around now and then.)

He wondered what Draco would do to the cerberus on watch if the Northman died. Or suicided! The hardened captain shuddered. (Absently he unlocked the door to Nils's cell and, sword in hand, stepped in to peer cautiously at the large covered body, the ruined eyes sunken in discolored sockets. When he backed out he somehow forgot to turn the key before withdrawing it.) If the Northman suicided on *his* watch, he told himself, he'd quickly follow him. But it would not happen.

Next he looked in on the star man, who lay curled in a ball, staring as unseeingly as if he'd been blinded too.

The weight from the big wall clock hung down about three decimeters, and he wound it back up. After midnight. A mental glance into the guard quarters found them all asleep, with no dreams worth watching. Briefly he considered waking them for an attack drill, but no, the man who *really* needed to be alert was the guard at the upper door. Yitzhak walked to the lower door and pulled the lever. When it had raised he walked thoughtfully up the three long flights of stairs. He had never before checked the upper door guard—that was the responsibility of the corridor patrol. But it was *his* bones if the man was caught off guard and someone else got hold of the speaker tube and tricked his way in.

For a moment he stood at the door, mind screened, hand on the latch lever, then threw it and pulled. The door swung open abruptly and the guard outside leaped back from it, fright in his eyes and ready sword in hand. The two orcs stared at each other, the guard recognizing the captain but uncertain and still ready to run him through. Standard procedure was to signal from below and inform him through the speaking tube.

What am I doing? Yitzhak thought suddenly. "You're awake I see," he said. "Good thing. If I ever catch you sleeping here . . ."

The guard leaked no thought, but his eyes . . . Yitzhak screened his embarrassment as best he could. Ahmed was dead, and no one else would engineer a breakout! What had he been thinking of? He'd made a fool of himself to the door guard!

Engaging the lock behind him, Yitzhak clopped back down the stairs. He needed a drink. The escape of a few nights ago, and the murder of the watch, must have thrust him deeper than he'd realized. The door guard thought he was a fool. He'd have to shut the dog's mouth before he spread the tale around. Maybe Hassan the Shark . . . Hassan owed him a favor, and he'd enjoy paying it in such a way.

By the time Yitzhak had returned to have his wine and make his plans, Nils was well inside the air duct that opened into the guard room wall. He didn't know where it led, except out of the dungeon. And there'd been the problem of getting into it. He'd had to jump from the heavy table at an opening he could see only through Ilse's psychic sight, and he wasn't coordinated to operate well that way. Then, with only a hand-hold to start with, he'd had to pull his bulky body into the small opening.

Inside he wriggled six meters to where it ended

in a cross duct, then paused to rest. The ordeal of
pain and shock and the demands of healing had
weakened him. There Ilse whispered in his mind.
While he'd been crawling, she had scouted the
ventilator system to its roof opening. He needed to
turn left. In such cramped space, that took effort.
Ilse was gone again, back to her body; there had
been a sense of urgency in her.

He pulled himself along, feeling without eyes
the utter blackness. Before long the duct opened
into a vertical shaft about a meter square. He
stood up in it, leaned his upper back against one
side, placed his bare feet against the other, and
began working his way upward.

Ilse was back. "I can only stay for a moment,"
she thought to him. "I'm in labor and it's coming
fast. I . . ." She was gone, drawn by the pain in her
body.

Fifteen grueling meters higher, his shoulders felt
the edge of another side duct entering the shaft; he
slid into it and rested. After several minutes he
continued upward, stopping in yet another duct
not far above.

Ilse was with him again. "Rest well here," she
told him. "There won't be another chance and you
have a long way to climb. The top is in a roof
garden. When you get out, circle the shaft—it's
like a chimney—keeping one hand on it and reaching out low with the other. You'll find a low-
walled thing of soil there, with thick bushes growing
in it. Crawl beneath the bushes and hide. I'll try to
have someone come down and get you."

He was alone again. Wriggling back into the
shaft, he started climbing. Warm air moved softly
upward around his sweating body. His shoulders

soon were raw from rubbing on rough dry stone; his legs and back were tired again. It was far. The dungeon was deep underground and the roofs high. He could not rest braced within the shaft; it would take strength to stay in place, draining his energy without progress. His sense of time blurred as he labored upward; there was only long concentration, and pain, and growing fatigue. Very largely he could put himself outside the pain, but exhaustion progressively slowed him.

At length he *had* to stop. There was no way to tell how much farther it was. With an effort of will he gathered himself, then jacked himself higher, half a meter, a meter.

And smelled fresh air! In moments his back-pressed head reached an opening.

The shaft was capped and the side-ports small. He reached an arm out, and then the other, exhaling and pushing powerfully with his legs to force his chest through. After pausing for a moment on the small of his back, he grasped the cap of the shaft, pulled, wriggled, and tumbled to the roof. For scant seconds he lay there, greasy with sweat, then turned over and crouched. There was no watchfulness nearby—no mind of any kind except for insects and sleeping birds. The planter was in front of him, fragrant with blossoms, and after standing for a moment, Nils crawled beneath its cool-leaved shrubs, to lay on the dry-surfaced soil.

A part of him watched while he slept.

The hull was on one-way transparent and Ram reached out to the instrument panel. Although it was against safety regulations, he pressed the key that slid the door open, to feel the air.

The City swung closer beneath, its rows of buildings defined by black shadow and the weak light of a slender, newly-risen moon. This was night on a planet, not the perpetual blackness of space, and it felt rich and beautiful, with an unreal reality that tingled. There were people down there, too, breathing, sleeping, dreaming—people whose existence was not quite real to him.

The whole scene felt unreal; he was acting in a dream fantasy at the request of his own hostage. Perhaps she had hypnotized him; the story she'd told between contractions sounded like sheerest lunacy. Though Celia had urged him, she hadn't needed to. This was action, something to do about something, something to accomplish after the waiting and frustration.

He maneuvered by thin moonlight rather than radar. The palace was easy to find, its tower and multiple roofs rising well above the buildings around. The cover of night wouldn't last long; it might be he could see a suggestion of dawn already, a possible lightness on the northeastern horizon. And it wouldn't do to be seen, to be associated with the escape. They still had hostages down there, unless they were dead.

Their spiral had brought them down until the tower loomed above them as they circled. Ram leveled off, gave the controls to his copilot, and crouched in the door. How in the world do you find a man hiding in the night beneath a bush on one of a multiplicity of roof gardens? A man that can't see you?

"Nils! Nils Järnhann!" he called with his mind. Penthouses, planters, small trees and shadowed shrubs swung silently beneath, and the man at the controls took her lower while Ram's eyes strained to see. "Nils! Nils Järnhann!"

"Here!" The answering thought was faint but distinct.

Ram commanded the copilot and they stopped, locked on a gravitic vector.

"Where?"

"Here!"

This time Ram was ready for the answer, and his psi-sense gave him a bearing on the silent call. He moved to the controls himself, silently slid *Beta* into position twenty meters above a roof, then gave them up again. From the door he saw a figure step out of shadow.

"I see him," he said quietly, and closed the switch that lowered the short flight of landing steps. "There! See? Take her down slowly until I say stop."

The barbarian stood like a statue, face aimed at the open door as the *Beta* settled. Ram knew the man was orienting himself through *his* eyes.

"Stop," Ram murmured, and crouched on the upper step. The air was sweet here, with a fragrance like pink lularea. He kept his eyes directed at the Northman to guide him, and could see the darkness of sunken sockets. A chill passed through him. The man moved deliberately to the ladder, reached for the hand rails, and pulled himself onto it with startlingly muscular arms. Ram reached out to him, their hands met, and he backed into the cabin with Ilse's husband following. Goose flesh crawled on the captain's skin.

The door slid shut and Ram stood in the darkness smelling the barbarian's stale sweat. There was something different in it, a taint that some long-buried memory in Ram's mind identified. It told of terrible injury and pain. The body seemed strong now but the odor lingered.

"You're a father," Ram said quietly. "It's a healthy girl. Willi, let's get our tails out of here before someone spots us."

XXIII

Kniven låg i slappa sommen,
söv på sidan a sin stridshäss,
söv iblann sin drömna kjämper
slumranne på stilla sletten
i d' lägren trygg å sikker,
slutan om a vakna posser
å a smylla hässpatryller.

I knivens panna pette viske,
snydde vä å blåste drömen
bort, då satt han upp å stärde.
Ingen vaken såg de önar.
Plyssli i d' mörka natten,
någon vita, jenomsynli,
vista sej t' Knivens springor.
Såg han mäkti Järnhanns spöke,
kjennte Ynglingen i ånnen
viskanne i sjäänli stillen.

[Listi lay relaxed and sleeping,
lay beside his horse in slumber,
lay among his dreaming warriors
sleeping on the silent prairie

in their war camp strong, protected,
guarded round by watchful sentries
and by stealthy scouts on horseback.

In his mind there came a whisper,
touched and broke his fragile dreaming,
sat up then and looked about him.
Nothing waking caught his vision.
Then within the darkness flickered
something thinly white, transparent.
As he stared with eyes thin-slitted,
saw the ghost of mighty Ironhand,
saw the spirit of the Youngling
whispering in the starlit stillness.]

From—THE JÄRNHANN SAGA,
Kumalo translation.

"Nils! Have you seen her?"

"Yes, through Ram's eyes before I slept. She's beautiful. Not all red like many newborn."

Ilse held out her hands and he took them, smiling down at her. "Darling," he said, "you are as remarkable at growing a baby as at every other thing."

Celia left them, closing the door behind her while the two conversed silently in a rich and subtle mixture of images, feelings, and unspoken words. After a bit Ilse showed him how to leave his body. He lay down on the deck of the small sick-room and after a minute she could not detect him; only his body was there. Then he returned.

"Was he aware of you at all?" she asked.

"Not consciously."

"His mind is tense and inward," she said, "and

easily threatened. Mostly he allows his psi to function only with verbalized thoughts, and that only guardedly.

"And your sight—could you see when you were out of the body?"

"Better than with eyes. More finely, and in every direction at once."

She nodded. "And now?"

"I'm going to the two star men, Matthew and Mikhail, and see how things are with them—what the situation is."

Concentrating but without effort he edged into thereness until he could see Matthew. He sensed at once the familiar feel of Draco's dungeon, which he had not expected. He'd assumed they were Ahmed's prisoners, and it had been clear earlier that Draco and Ahmed were enemies. Scanning, he sensed Mikhail nearby, the still catatonic Chandra, and a female with Chandra, desolate and in pain, that had to be the one called Anne Marie. The hostages had been brought together.

A dungeon captain, ill-at-ease, psi intent, was moving sword in hand down the alleyway between the rows of cells, and Nils withdrew. For only a minute he stayed in his body, sensing Ilse's awareness, then left again.

Nephthys was alone at her loom, looking critically at a half-completed tapestry. She was conscious of him almost at once. Carefully she looked around, saw nothing meaningful, and took her lip thoughtfully between her teeth.

"I'm not asleep," she thought. "Is it you? Can the dead return?"

He acknowledged that it was him. "Is the one called Ahmed still alive?" he asked.

"No. Draco had him killed and rules the entire army now." She hesitated. "Do you know about your people?"

"What about them?"

"Ahmed made an alliance with them. Oh Nils, I heard they'd blinded you but I didn't know you'd been killed."

"They blinded me." His mind was gentle but persistent. "What about my people?"

"They sent out an army to help Ahmed overthrow Draco. Ahmed had promised to protect them with his sky chariot if Draco tried to attack them in the open. They believed if Ahmed won he'd take us all to Egypt and leave this country to them. But now . . ."

She paused and he finished for her. "And now Draco has the sky chariot and the whole orc army and plans to destroy us."

Mentally she nodded.

"When?"

"I don't know. As soon as his army reaches them. It left this morning."

She looked around her again.

"I can see you now, barely, as if you were made of pale light. Can you let me see you better?"

He made a stronger facsimile of his body until it appeared almost like flesh. Nephthys reached toward him and touched . . . nothing. "Can't you take me in your arms then?"

Gentle negative.

"You have sons. Two of them." She walked to a slender silvered cord and somewhere a bell rang. Nils withdrew to near absence, and in a moment a servant entered.

"Bring the babies," Nephthys ordered.

The slave girl curtsied and left. In three minutes she was back, pushing a large-wheeled crib of simple elegance, and left it. Somewhat, Nils reappeared.

"They are not light-skinned like you," Nephthys said, "but they have hair."

Nils smiled softly in her mind.

"I wish they could have known you." She was suddenly forlorn. The response she read in him had nothing of regret or unhappiness, only a soft awareness akin to love. He began to fade.

"When Draco comes back from killing your people, he will die," Nephthys thought after him. "I promise you."

He was gone.

Nils conveyed to Ilse what he had learned, then got up from the deck. "I need your help to bathe," he said. "I smell of injury and old sweat."

Ilse sat up and put her feet on the floor. "I'll take you to a bathing place; they call it a 'shower.' It is very pleasant; you can have the water as warm or cold as you want. Come, I'll help you."

For lack of clothes to fit him, someone had cut and hemmed a sort of toga from a bed sheet until something better could be sewn. The man looked, Ram thought, like an artist's conception of Alaric, the Visigoth chief, after his barbarians had sacked Rome. Alaric with his skull shaved and grown to disreputable stubble. Alaric with empty sockets ugly in his face. He'd have to have eye patches made.

"It's time we talked about getting Nikko Kumalo back from your people," the captain said brusquely.

"It's time to get all your people back."

Easily said, Ram thought cynically, then reminded himself that this was a man who had escaped a dungeon while naked, unarmed, and blind.

"Get them back? How?"

"Land your pinnace on the roof where you picked me up, close to the air chimney so it will be inside your shield. Then send men down on a rope and bring the prisoners up."

"Aren't there armed guards down below? I can't risk sending men into that!"

"Let some of my people go down. It's their nature and pleasure to fight."

"It's no one's nature to fight—not in mortal combat!"

"It's some people's nature."

"And what if the orcs come in the *Alpha* and attack us while we're sitting on the roof? We wouldn't have a chance. All we could do would be to sit there inside the shield. And the orcs would think of things, like attacking the commast to make us pull it in, and then sending smoke up the ventilator. Then we'd have to deactivate, and they'd hit us with grenades from the *Alpha* before we could get away."

Nils flowed admiration at the man's quick mind, but Ram could not accept admiration now, so the Northman eased off, saying, "That couldn't happen if you captured or destroyed the *Alpha* first."

Ram stared at him.

"There were two orc armies," Nils continued, "one ruled by Ahmed, the other by Draco. The two men were deadly rivals. Ahmed made an offer to my people: if they would help him attack Draco, then when he'd won control, he'd take the orcs to another land and leave the country to us. Now, my people wouldn't willingly meet a large army in open grassland where orc numbers could over-whelm them. But Ahmed promised to use the *Alpha* to keep Draco from riding out against them.

"And they agreed.

"But somehow Draco overthrew Ahmed, and the entire orc army left the city today to attack my people, and the *Alpha* will also attack them.

"The men in the *Alpha* will be looking and think-ing downward, not upward. They think of you as cowardly and will hardly expect you to attack. That would be a good time to strike with the *Beta*. If you succeed, you could borrow warriors from my people to raid the dungeon.

"You are not used to war and violence, and ruthlessness is foreign and terrible to you, so natu-rally you feel uncertain and afraid. But you are a man who's faced and overcome difficulties before. You helped build this star ship, and that was not easy. If you concentrate on how to take the *Alpha*, you may very well succeed. The advantage is yours, because you know what your, your science, is able to do."

Ram's face reflected a hardening commitment now, a decision made. "All right," he said, "I'll do it. I think I already see how; I just need to work out the details. Meanwhile I'll have someone take you down to your people to warn them."

"No, I can go myself without a pinnace, the way Ilse went to help me and the way I went back to the city today and learned what I just told you."

Ram was jarred inwardly by Nils's words. It hadn't occurred to him to wonder how this man had gotten his information. *Damn! I shouldn't have overlooked that*, he told himself. *In this world of savages I'm a baby, credulous and naive.*

But I'm damned well also a first-class engineer, and there's no one at all down there to match what I can do with that.

At 3,500 meters the pinnace cruised slowly, as if gloating, checking the progress of the Northman army. It was a loose assemblage of mounted platoons covering many hectares of plain, conspicuous to the naked eye even though yesterday's rain had laid the dust.

A second pinnace sledded out of the sun behind the first, braking sharply as she approached; her pilot was not an experienced gunner and couldn't expect a second chance if he wasted his first. A shimmer in the target told him its hull was on one-way transparent, increasing the risk that he'd be seen. Even so he continued slowing, relying on the sun to hide him. At thirty meters his sights would coincide exactly with his line of fire. He rode his sights in, thumb poised, until at thirty-five meters their focus sharpened suddenly. He hit the makeshift firing stud, sticked back and banked sharply.

A hundred meters to starboard now the *Alpha* still floated as she had.

"We did it!" the pilot said. "We must have! Otherwise she'd be taking evasive action. Ivan, get ready to board."

Ivan nodded, pulled a mask over his face and adjusted the straps. "Okay, Willi, I'm as ready as I'll ever be. I just hope this mask works like it's supposed to."

"It will. Dr. Uithoudt tested it herself."

"Okay. But let's be careful with me, huh? I'm a motor tech, not a bloody daredevil."

The *Beta* moved delicately alongside *Alpha*, matching speeds. Ivan Yoshida leaned far out, reaching, the other hand gripping tightly to a rail, slapped a magnetic disk on the hull alongside, and then another. A line ran from each disk to his belt. "There must be a better way to do this," he muttered, then called, "Move a little closer—half a meter."

Willi gave him a few centimeters. After taking up the slack in his safety lines, Ivan jumped, landing with his feet against the *Alpha's* hull, and *Beta* drew away, ahead and to starboard. Some highly toxic gas would come out of *Alpha* when Ivan activated the door.

They saw the panel slide back, and after a short pause to peer inside, Ivan pulled himself in. A minute later his voice came from the radio. "All dead in here except me. You not only socked her in the air intake; you must have put her right down the nostril. The way the fan sounds, she penetrated the control unit and rammed part of it into the circulator. I turned it off so she wouldn't burn out."

"Okay. Better leave the door open then, speed her up, and fly around for a few minutes before you start down. That'll blow her out more than good enough. And it wouldn't hurt to run up the commast and turn the snorkel on. Just don't be in any hurry to take off your mask."

Willi turned to the silent Northman seated by the aft bulkhead. "I'll call the ship now, Nils, and tell them we've got *Alpha* back. That'll make the skipper happy. Then, if you're ready, we'll go down and get on with it."

*   *   *

The Northmen stopped and sat their horses casually as they watched the two pinnaces settle half a kilometer ahead of the lead elements. Then Kniv Listi, Sten Vannaren, and four others walked their horses toward the landing spot.

Beta touched down and Willi Loo activated the door and landing steps. "Help Nils, Charley." The other man guided the blind warrior, although he no longer needed help.

"That's sure a pretty prairie," Willi said to no one in particular. "I wish my dad could see it. He loves good land." He touched the send switch again. "Ivan, when you set *Alpha* down, activate your shield, drag the bodies out, shift a hundred meters or so and reactivate. Then check out the damage to the circulator, and any other possible damage the rocket may have done."

Charles DuBois was coming back up the steps and Willi activated his shield. Six Northmen were riding up to Nils, and the audio pickup brought the tonal unintelligibility of their speech. One dismounted and led his horse while he walked beside Nils; all seven went to the *Alpha* and watched Ivan unload. When he'd lifted again they inspected the corpses.

He'd heard they scalped their enemies, but they did not bother with these.

Meanwhile a second party of six Northmen had ridden up to *Beta's* shield. Five dismounted and tied their reins to a leather rope held by the sixth. The five wore swords but had left their shields attached to their saddles. These must be the ones, Willi thought, the rescue commando. They were grinning as if they really looked forward to it; there was no trace of grimness.

Nils and the group with him were returning now, and they too grinned. Willi eyed Kniv Listi and guessed it was he who commanded this army; but the insignia he wore were his eyes, his body, his bearing, and maybe subtler things. He looked not cruel, not even unfriendly. But hard. *I wouldn't want to tangle with that one*, Willi thought. *He looks like he could disembowel a man with his fingertips.*

"One of the dead men is Draco, the orc ruler," Nils called. "Maybe Ram would like to know that. Send Charles out to us now. I'm going over the plan with the rescue party, and he should listen. Sten will translate for him. Then, if Ivan is ready, we'll load and get started. And tell Ram I'll fly with you instead of in the *Alpha*."

"With me? Then who'll guide the rescue party?"

"I can leave my body with you as surety and still guide the raiders. I will project my spirit so that they can see it, and hear my thoughts. Ram has misgivings, because once our warriors are aboard the *Alpha*, they could take it over if they decided to, and your people with it. But if I'm with you in the *Beta*, then *I* am *his* hostage."

It all sounded strange to Willi, regardless of which pinnace Nils was on. He'd heard how Nils was supposed to have escaped, and that he'd come down in the spirit to plan with the Northmen, but that didn't make it feel real. On the other hand it didn't distress him. Willi was a very practical engineer; his ultimate criterion was not how well something fitted his pre-existing notions, or its explainability. It was its workability that counted. And this blind man, by whatever means, had escaped a guarded dungeon.

Ivan," he said into the radio, "come over and be ready to take on the troops. Nils will stay with me, but he says he'll still be able to guide you."

There was a pause. "Huh! Well, I guess that's not much weirder than if he was here with me, considering . . . How's he going to manage that? I'm no telepath."

"You'll have to wait and see, I guess. He seems totally confident about it. Captain Uithoudt, have you followed this transmission?"

"Affirmative. What was that about Nils staying with you?"

"He says you'll feel better having him in our control when his warriors are occupying *Alpha* with some of our people."

Ram grunted. He *had* felt concern, but he wasn't sure how much this relieved it. "All right," he said. "Just make sure you *are* in control."

Of one thing Ram was certain. He was committed, done with waiting, and he wasn't going to back down now.

When the two pinnaces had taken off, the Northman army began to move. They didn't continue eastward however. Two platoons of warriors turned back in the direction they'd come from. The remainder, roughly eight hundred warriors and one thousand bowmen, divided into two equal forces. Half rode north, the other south.

XXIV

The city appeared on the horizon and seemed to move toward them, spreading, the black tower dominant even at a distance, marking the palace. *And now what?* Ivan thought. He glanced at Charles DuBois sitting beside him, wiry, muscular, the perennial handgun champion at the Deep Harbor harvest games. Sidearms were belted to his waist now and the pockets of his mechanic's coveralls bulged with grenades. The man's hobby was guns and his reading was of war. Probably he'd regretted living on New Home instead of, say, twentieth-century Earth.

Ivan reduced their air speed as they approached the first rows of buildings, and suddenly he was aware of something between Charles and himself. The Northman knelt there, or seemed to, and on the other side of him—through him—he saw Charles staring narrowly.

"Go slower and circle the tower not far above the higher roofs," Nils instructed. The voice was not a voice, Ivan realized; it spoke within his mind. He cut both speed and altitude and swung around the tower.

"Closer and slower. Then look down and watch for me." And he was gone. Seconds later Ivan saw him atop a ventilator cap, and floated down beside it, not quite landing. Nils disappeared. Charles jumped out, hurriedly placed four small charges, and jumped back aboard. The pinnace veered away some seventy meters, there was a sharp blast, and the ventilator cap spun into the air, accompanied by shards of rock and pieces of mortar.

Quickly Ivan moved the pinnace back to the spot, landed, and activated the shield. Speed was important now. Charles was out again, with a collapsible tripod, and swiftly began setting it up, its pulley over the shaft opening. The six Northmen crouched in the pinnace, still grinning, waiting.

Nils was there again. "It's not blocked," he said, gesturing at the shaft. "They don't know how I got out. The noise alarmed them just now in the guard room, but they don't know what it was or what it means. I'll go back down and distract the guard officer. The longer it is before they know what's happening, the less chance they'll have to bring in more soldiers."

He disappeared again.

Charles pulled slender cable off a winch newly bolted to the pinnace deck. It had loops at five-meter intervals. "All right, out!" he said to Sten, who gestured to the other Northmen. Ivan knelt by the winch control and watched first Charles and then the Northmen start one by one down the shaft. The last two were still on top when orcs came streaming from a stairway onto the roof with swords drawn, charging the pinnace and ventilator. The first several crashed into the unseen shield as into a stone wall, falling back stunned. Those behind stopped short and stood uncertainly, their eyes shifting from the final disappearing Northman to the pinnace door, through which they could see the kneeling Ivan. Their leader spoke sharply. Two of his men trotted to the head of the open stairs and out of sight. Then he looked thoughtfully at the commast: Ivan moved to the panel and lowered it to safety.

At the bottom of the shaft, Charles crawled quickly into the narrow horizontal duct. Nils was waiting at the junction ahead and directed him into the branch that led to the guard room. The eyeless Northman was a pale light that illuminated nothing; the walls of the duct were as black as if he wasn't there. When Charles had negotiated the turn and started toward the opening, he heard an angry voice ahead, with a tone of command.

"The guard captain is a telepath," Nils whispered in his mind. "He's sensed you; be ready. They'll shoot arrows into the duct as soon as they see anything."

A cold hand had gripped Charles' gut as he crawled. Now it turned to a feeling of utter paralysis through which somehow he continued to crawl forward. The square of light ahead grew quickly until it was an opening almost within reach of his hand.

And almost miraculously the fear disappeared. Now he felt only calm and alert, quick and strong. He lay there long enough for the warriors to close up behind him, at the same time pulling a grenade from a pocket. Sten squeezed his foot. He pulled the pin, let the safety lever snap free, and deliberately counted to three before awkwardly tossing the grenade through the opening. An arrow zipped into the duct and rebounded, slicing his calf with its sharp-edged head, and there was an explosion in the guard room. Quickly, furiously, he scrambled head-first into the opening, and, without taking time to look or think, he rolled onto his back and pulled his upper body out with his hands. Sten grasped his feet and pushed, and in one spasmodic moment he was being lowered head-first, then dropped. The stone floor crashed into him, striking his extended hands, then his back, and he rolled to his knees beside a shattered orc, drawing his autopistol. An orc in a doorway was pulling his bowstring. Charles snapped a shot, and saw him fall as the arrow struck the high ceiling.

There was an instant's silence, then a thud and a grunt and Sten rolled into him. Instantly the Northman was on his feet, reaching up to help the next man who was sliding out of the duct, back arched, like some grotesque steel-mailed myth birthing from a stone womb. A hurried arrow darted from the doorway, striking Sten's steel cap and deflecting. Charles fired three more rounds, drew a second grenade, let the safety go, then fired another short burst as he rushed and pitched the grenade around the corner of the door. It roared, fragments whirred, and he darted in. There were cots and fallen men. One man was still on his feet against a wall, eyes and mouth wide, and he shot him down.

The key! He was supposed to get the key! Charles ran out again, saw an orc with a breastplate sprawled by the table, knelt, and shot off the ring that held the single large key to his belt.

There were shouts then, like voices in a well, words neither Anglic nor Scandinavian, and two of the Northmen ran past him into a short corridor toward the sound, swords in their hands. He started after them.

"No!" The wraith of Nils cut him off. "The other way! Quickly! The corridor to your left, and let your people out of their cells!"

For just a second he hesitated, confused, staring after the two warriors, then turned, dodged another rushing Northman, and ran with the key in his hand. But behind his eyes was what he'd started toward a moment before—orcs, a mass of orcs spilling through a doorway and the two Northmen hacking at them. He'd be killed. They all would. They were trapped down here like rats.

"Here!" The wraith was ahead of him again, pointing. Charles thrust the key into a lock and turned it.

"Watch now. There are two more farther on— Matthew and Mikhail. Quickly!"

The two men were at their cell doors, amazement in their eyes as Charles ran up and let them out. They started down the corridor, stopping to obey when a ghost called to them to help Chandra and Anne Marie.

Charles sprinted past them, pushing a fresh magazine into his pistol grip, then brought out another grenade. Pulling the pin with his teeth, he careened through the guard room and into the corridor where the two Northmen had been fighting.

It was over. Three Northmen stood there now by a litter of bodies. A heavy iron door had dropped into the opening from which the orcs had been issuing, nearly severing some bodies that lay across the threshold. Sten leaned grimly on a lever near it, a bloody sword in his hand. Three of the dead were Northmen.

Charles realized he had an armed grenade in his hand, walked back through the guard room and peered into the room with the cots. An orc knelt there, wounded, trying to stem the flow of blood from a comrade with the corner of a blanket.

Damn! thought Charles. *No place to throw the damned thing. What in the hell do I do with . . .* Abruptly the kneeling orc was on his feet, a knife in his hand, and Charles as quickly shot him, then backed from the room and lobbed the grenade around the edge of the doorway. The five seconds were forever before it exploded.

In the guard room, Matthew and Mikhail stood beside Anne Marie, staring at a Northman scalping an orc. Matthew had the slack-bodied Chandra over his shoulder. The other two Northmen strode in, hands and wrists smeared red.

"Let's get out of here," Charles said urgently, "before something happens."

Sten looked at him, nodded, and gave an order in Scandinavian. They moved the heavy guard-room table beneath the ventilator. One Northman was boosted up and pulled himself into the duct. Then one after another they all were helped until only Sten was left to jump for it.

When they were gone, the only sound was the soft moaning of a twice wounded orc still alive in the guard quarters. The prisoners in their cells were as silent as if a threatening guard might come momentarily and punish them.

XXV

"*Alpha*, this is the captain. *Alpha*, this is the captain. Over."

"This is *Alpha*. Over."

"Ivan, have you returned the Northman raiders yet? Over."

"Not yet, Captain. We've been overflying the two armies—the orcs and the Northmen—at about six kilometers. The Northman in charge of the commando—his name is Sten—is sizing the situation up, seeing where the armies are relative to one another and to the Danube. And man, let me tell you, there's an awful lot of orcs down there. Must outnumber the Northmen eight or ten to one, and . . ."

"*Damn* it, Ivan! I didn't send you down there to carry out a military reconnaissance! Your orders were to get our people back and bring them up here! Unload those Northmen as fast as you can and get our people back to the *Phaeacia*; they may need medical attention critically! Have you got that straight?"

"Right, Captain. Sorry. Nobody seemed that critical, and I figured that five minutes . . ."

"ARE YOU A MEDIC?!?!" Ram's voice was suddenly shrill. "Who told you you could make medical decisions?" The violence of his own reaction startled and shook him.

"Yes, sir. I'm on my way to unload the Northmen at once, sir."

"Let me talk to him," Matthew said softly. "*Phaeacia*, this is Matt Kumalo. Over."

There was a brief lag, and the voice, when it answered, was husky and earnest. "God but I'm glad to hear your voice, Matt. How are you? How are all of you?"

"Mike and I seem to be all right, Ram, considering. And Anne Marie says she's all right too. But I expect Jomo and Celia had better check us over when we get back up. Chan's the one in bad shape. Catatonic. He was curled up in a tight ball when Charles and the Northmen got us out, and I had to clip him pretty hard to loosen him up enough to carry."

"Okay. Sounds like it could be worse," Ram said. "Look, Matt, about the *Alpha*: I'm really concerned that we don't get mixed up in their war down there. What I want is to get all of us back on board, including Nikko."

"We're already mixed up in their war, Ram," Matthew said mildly, "or maybe I should say they're mixed up in ours. Three Northmen were killed getting us out of that hell-hole—three out of six."

There were seconds of silence. "It was their choice," Ram answered. "They like that kind of thing; they wanted to go. And I didn't plan to tell you yet, but the Northmen are holding Nikko hostage."

This time the communication lag was Matthew's. "Hostage?"

"To pressure me for help when the orcs had the *Alpha*. But we've got Ilse and her baby of course, and Nils is on board the *Beta*. So now that we've got *Alpha* away from the orcs we ought to be able to trade and get Nikko back."

"Ilse's husband on board the *Beta*? Are you sure? I'd swear he was dead. This may sound crazy, but everyone else seemed to see what I did—Mike and Anne Marie did anyway. His *ghost* was in the dungeon during the fighting."

"I believe you, all right, but he's not dead. It's just something he seems to do, some wild psi talent. Ilse does it too."

Ivan interrupted. "Matt, you'd better sit down now. I'm going to land in just a minute. Sten says their big chief is down below."

"Right. Did you hear that, Ram?"

"I heard it."

Beta was in sight now, a bit above them, as if she'd been waiting; she made no move to land. *Alpha* sat down gently. Charles opened the door and sent the landing steps out. At once two powerful arms wrapped tightly around him from behind, pinning his arms to his sides, and carried him helpless from the pinnace. A second Northman picked up Anne Marie and carried her unprotestingly out. Quickly Ivan activated the shield.

"You're trapped," he said. "I turned the shield on; you can't get out."

"Then turn it off," Sten said reasonably.

"I thought we were friends," Matthew said. "What are you doing this for?"

"We need your sky boat. Don't worry; we're not orcs. We won't hurt you. Get out now—"He gestured at Mikhail. "—you and him, and take the unconscious one with you."

Matthew looked at the Northman's scarred face for a moment, finding neither threat nor relenting in it. "Okay," he said, turning. "Help me, Mike." They picked Chandra up and carried him outside.

Sten and Ivan were alone then. "Open your invisible wall so we can take them away," Sten instructed. "Then do what is needed for me to talk to Nils Järnhann in the other sky boat."

Ivan hesitated and the Northman's sword slid from its scabbard to touch lightly on a switch, deactivating the shield. Ivan's eyes caught on the congealed blood that remained where the blade met the handguard. Obviously the Northman's attention missed little, and his competence and willingness were beyond doubt.

"*Beta* and *Phaeacia*, this is Ivan. *Beta* and *Phaeacia*, this is Ivan. The Northmen have taken us prisoner. The Northmen have taken all of us on the *Alpha* prisoner and one of them wants to talk to Nils now. Over."

Willi broke in from the *Beta*. "Captain, this is Willi. Captain, this is Willi. Okay to let Nils talk to him? Over."

Long seconds passed without answer.

"*Phaeacia*, this is *Beta*. *Phaeacia*, this is *Beta*. Are you receiving? Are you . . ."

"*Let the goddamned savages talk to each other!*"

The anger was like a hammer, shaking the spacemen, but after a moment Sten began speaking calmly in Scandinavian; Nils answered in the same language. After several minutes Nils switched to Anglic.

"Captain Uithoudt, this is Nils. Sten says he and our war chief, Kniv Listi, want both pinnaces to help them fight the orcs. He says the man called Charles is skilled with your weapons and they want him to teach some of our people so they can shoot orcs from the sky when the battle comes."

Again the reply came after a long pause. "And what if I tell him to go to hell?"

"Hell?"

"Hell! What if I refuse to give him the *Beta*?"

"He says the army will take your people with them, and if the army is destroyed, the orcs will kill or recapture your people. But if we have the pinnaces to help us, we will surely win, and your people will be safe."

Again there was no immediate answer. Ivan got nervous but Sten seemed relaxed enough.

"I'll go this far," Ram said at last. "Your people already have the *Alpha*, so I'll agree to let Ivan fly it for them and Charles can show them how to shoot and use grenades. But I won't give up the *Beta*. I'll let her fly air support—that is, I'll let her fight the orcs—but she'll have no Northmen on board. My own people will fly her and do the shooting. Under no conditions will I let the *Beta* out of my control. Over."

Nils and Sten conversed briefly.

"Captain," said Nils, "Kniv agrees to your offer. Also he will let the *Beta* pick up two of your people, Anne Marie and Chandra. He says the woman is sick and the man should not die among strangers.

He says the *Beta* will not be molested when it lands.''

"Hah! Why should I believe that?"

"Has one of us lied to you?"

"What assurance can you give me?"

"Assurance?"

"Pledge," Ram said, patiently now. "What pledge can you give me that your people won't try to take over the *Beta* when she picks up Chan and Anne?"

"We are offering you two of your people back, the two you were most worried about. My people will stand well away when Willi picks them up. And finally I give you this oath. If they don't let the *Beta* fly away freely with your people, I will take my own life, or you can take it if you prefer. I have said it. Over."

Sten spoke quietly to Kniv, who narrowed his eyes and nodded.

Ram's voice was little more than a hoarse whisper. "Willi, land and pick up Chan and Anne Marie, and bring them up immediately. And be careful. Call me as soon as you're off the ground with them. Over."

"Right, Captain. I'm to land, pick up Chan and Anne, and bring them to the ship immediately. And call you as soon as I'm off the ground again. Yes, sir."

"Affirmative. *Phaeacia* over and out."

"*Beta* out."

Ram pushed open the dispensary door almost violently, his expression so bitter it frightened his wife.

"Welcome home! Welcome back to Earth!" he said, glaring at her. "If I ever get them all back on board I'll leave this rotten planet so fast it'll make your bloody head swim!"

XXVI

And it came to pass . . . that the Lord cast down
great stones from heaven upon them unto Aze-
kah, and they died: they were more which died
with hailstones than they whom the children of
Israel slew with the sword.

HOLY BIBLE, *Joshua 10: 10.*

There was no longer even a semblance of a road,
and on the high plain they needed none. Their
formation was a great oblong checkerboard of cavalry units several hours into the morning's ride,
with the dew now dried by the sun.

A scout trotted his horse toward them, riding
smoothly, proudly erect, sunlight glinting on
plumed and polished helmet and black mail, upright lance tilted a correct ten degrees forward.
Another orc detached himself from the small lead
formation and galloped to meet him.

Kamal had been experiencing misgivings; something seemed to have gone wrong, perhaps seriously.
Draco had not contacted him all of yesterday, either directly or by radio, which was disturbing in

itself. As a consequence he'd had no information of the enemy in that time. Judging from the last report, he'd expected to meet the Northmen before noon today, and in fact before now. He'd even made camp early the day before, to help ensure they'd not meet in the evening.

Having decided the preceding evening that he could not rely on aerial reconnaissance, he'd sent scouts out before dawn to fan widely through the countryside ahead. With one of them returning now, his concern was replaced by hard-eyed attentiveness. His aide-de-camp rode back with the scout at heel.

"They've found where the Northmen were."

"Were? So they learned about us and turned back! We'll have to catch them then!"

The aide-de-camp turned to the scout and gestured for him to speak.

"They don't seem to have turned back, my Lord," the man said. "They split into two forces, one turning north, the other south. Yesterday, by the signs. We have riders following both groups."

"Yesterday! How far ahead was this?"

"About seven kilometers."

"How large a force? Their entire army?"

"I don't know, my Lord. A large one, surely; the grass was widely trampled."

So! And where was the high-flying Draco, the eye of the army? He wished now that Dov, in command of the City garrison, had been left a radio, but there were only three for the entire field army. He also wished for a few squads of horse barbarians, for scouts. They'd have told him how many Northmen had been there and when. It should have been fairly late in the day, for them to have gotten so far east, but one couldn't be sure, especially with Northmen. If they'd broken camp before dawn yesterday, or forced the march. . . . But why would they force their march? They were too smart to wear out their horses without good reason.

Now he had to decide in ignorance. He had the nasty feeling that the Northmen were in charge of the situation, maneuvering him into doing what they wanted; he'd had too much experience of them in the Ukraine. But how could they even know he was out here on the march? The sky chariot should have seen and killed any far-ranging Northman scouts or patrols.

And the sky chariot should have contacted him the evening before and again this morning.

He looked up as a rider approached at a canter, calling to him. "My Lord! Another scout is returning!"

Kamal squinted westward at the scout, still distant, and ordered out his aide-de-camp to meet him, while a trumpeter halted the army. Minutes later his aide galloped back hard, with something on his lance tip.

"My Lord!" he snapped, and held out a stinking severed head to his commander. "One of the scouts found the bodies of our Lord Draco and others near the place where the Northman army divided. He brought this as proof because the bodies had been stripped and there were no insignia."

"And the sky chariot?"

"Not there."

"Any sign of it?"

"He didn't say."

That was an answer of sorts. Had it been there, the scout would have told of it. But how else could Draco have gotten there? And yet, how could the

Northmen have moved it? Surely they couldn't fly it; it had taken training by the star men to enable Ahmed's men to fly them, and the Northmen were barbarians.

The scout was trotting up to them. "Man!" Kamal shouted at him, "don't you know anything except that they're dead?"

"Yes, my Lord. Their bodies bore no wounds. They had no marks of arrow, sword, or knife, and they had not been scalped."

Kamal swore, looking again at Draco's discolored face. The hair was still there, and the Northmen always scalped anyone they killed. "How many bodies?"

"Four, my Lord."

All four! "And no sign of the sky chariot?"

"None, my Lord."

Too many questions were unanswered; there were too many unknowns. But this he did know: he had to deal with the Northmen without help from the air.

"The army will turn back toward the City," he said finally. "Apparently the Northmen know about us and out-flanked us in the night. And there are only five cohorts left in the City in case they attack it."

It struck him then. Five cohorts—1,500 men. Draco had rough-counted the Northmen from the sky. Five cohorts were almost as many as the whole Northman army, and they were *orcs*—trained, disciplined, fighting *orcs*!

The neoviking mystique, their reputation for supernatural cunning and invincibility, had been overblown, he told himself. And Kamal had no respect for a commander whose automatic response to an enemy was caution, defense. Out here the Northmen had no forests to hide in or attack from, and they bled and died like other men. He'd killed one himself—skinned him and watched him die. Another he'd crucified, to groan to death beneath the Ukrainian sun.

He changed his decision, in part.

"We're between the Northmen and their people now, so the Third Legion won't go back with us. They'll continue to the mountains, to where the Northman army left its people, and wipe them out. They will take no prisoners except girl children and young women."

Kamal began to expand and glow as he continued. "Couriers to each legion. Inform the commanders. Have each of them signal when he's been informed. I will then signal the First, Second, and Fourth to begin the return. The Third will stand, and its commander will ride here to me for instructions. I'll catch up with the rest on their first break.

"Is that clear?"

It was, and the mnemonically trained couriers galloped off to repeat his instructions exactly. Within ten minutes the army was moving.

The men of the Third Legion considered themselves privileged. Instead of riding like the others to battle, they were riding to sport. When they stopped that evening, sentries were posted, and patrols circled the camp, but this was Standard Operating Procedure, not a response to possible danger. And rather than each man sleeping by his picketed horse, the animals were hobbled and picketed within a single large rope corral around which the men camped.

To the *Alpha's* infrared scanner the paddock was conspicuous in the night.

For the Northmen, archery was more than a lifelong sport and sometime tool of war. It had also been an important means of feeding themselves, and its use had developed in them a fine sense of general marksmanship. They knew and used without questioning the basic principle that the way to hit something was to have a target and intend to hit it, not questioning your ability.

Charles had explained the automatic rifles to the four men assigned to him, through the bilingual skill of Sten Vannaren, had demonstrated and given them some dry firing. Finally each had fired several short bursts, and their targets were quickly rags. Afterward, waiting, they'd dry-fired from the door of the grounded pinnace at imaginary orcs, shouting "da-da-da-da-da-da!" like little boys. Charles had grinned at the sound as he worked beneath the nose of the craft.

The targets beneath them now were live, but the barbarians felt no qualms. A floodlight from above startled the sentries; then automatic rifles roused the camp. Slowly the pinnace circled the paddock as two riflemen fired into the horse herd. When one had emptied his magazine he threw an H.E. grenade from the door while another man seated a new magazine in the rifle and took his place. Hobbled horses pulled their pickets, milling madly or crowhopping through the confused camp and into the open prairie.

The well-spaced orc patrols, circling two to three kilometers away, stopped in the darkness to stare at the distant light, listening to the strange and somehow dangerous sounds. In a general way they realized that the camp was being attacked, and fearful and isolated though each squad felt, they did not ride toward the disturbance.

The distant floodlight blinked out, the explosions stopped, and they felt their aloneness even more in the silent and unrelieved darkness.

The darkness did not hide them. To the *Alpha* they were bright clusters of oblong lights. The pinnace settled undetected above one patrol and two grenades were tossed out, one H.E. and one fragmentation. Then it moved silently on to the second. The patrols were victimized by their separation; only three of the ten realized what the occasional scattered blasts meant and whipped their horses at last toward the crowded anonymity of camp.

Nearly 3,000 orcs huddled in the night, too disciplined to panic, too shocked and bewildered to plan, afraid to go out and hunt their horses. Not until dawn did they round up their animals and count them. Nearly a hundred had been killed or disabled by the Northmen from the air. Hundreds more, wounded or dangerous with panic, had been killed by the orcs to still their frantic hooves. Many, in the open prairie, had been felled with swords by night-covered Northmen riders.

The legion could not seek help or advice; there had been neither radio nor psi-tuner to send with them, nor apparent need. The commander and his staff agreed; they could reach the shelter of foothill forests with two days of steady riding—with only one more night beneath the open sky. Then perhaps they still might carry out their mission.

The eight hundred and on foot might make it in four days of hard marching, but they'd be on their own. The men on horseback would not stay with them.

As the climbing sun began to heat the day, the orcs started westward again, heavy with foreboding. The prairie now seemed huge and hostile, with no help to be had, and home almost a four-day ride behind them. To go west, as they were, might be logical, but psychologically it was devastating. Especially to the men on foot as they saw the cavalry move farther and farther ahead and out of sight.

That same night the First, Second, and Fourth Legions had camped on the last extensive dry ground west of the Danube's old west channel. They numbered 7,300 instead of 9,000; the five cohorts guarding the City had been assigned from the Fourth Legion and were half of its roster.

The old west channel had long been merely a marsh, with a series of lakes and sloughs connected by flood channels. Between it and the river the country was mostly more marshes and wet meadows. Across the marshes the orcs had built a military road to the Danube, of squared stone slabs laid on gravel. It crossed flood channels and creeks on low causeways. On the east side of the river it continued again to the City. The river itself was not bridged; men customarily swam their horses across.

The Northmen had not taken this road, and again Kamal was puzzled and mistrusting. They had followed instead an old road southeastward. This second route was really a cattle trail located to take advantage of what firm ground there was, filled with broken rock in the worst places, with a rough causeway over the main flood channel. It reached the river about six kilometers upstream of the military road, at rough stone docks. The dock location took advantage of the current in barging cattle to the City via the ancient ship canal.

It was disturbing when a shrewd and deadly enemy did the illogical for an unknown reason. It smelled of trickery. The best explanation Kamal could think of was that the Northmen feared meeting a strong orc force on the military road—feared being caught between armies where the marshes would frustrate their freedom of movement. They would have to abandon their horses in order to flee.

That was probably it, Kamal decided, and felt better. The Northmen were always wary of traps and couldn't know there wasn't another orc army. Kamal sent a light scouting patrol pounding down the Northmen's trail while his army rested their mounts. Three hours later they returned on lathered horses. The Northmen, they reported, had followed the route to the river and entered it below the docks.

Kamal still wasn't sure, but now this was beginning to smell like the overdue stroke of luck that could ensure success. For where the Northmen had crossed would put them on the *South* side of the ship canal, and the City was on the north side. When they discovered this they'd have another crossing to make, an impossible crossing. The bridge above the City was easily defended, and its center section could be raised. As for fording, the canal's smooth current was strong, and except for easily defended boat landings, its sides were too steep for horses.

He had his trumpeter signal a speed march. Thousands of horses began an easy trot, taking the military, not the cattle, road. Within an hour Kamal was at the river, its dark water nearly a kilometer wide. Nagged again by misgivings, the grim-faced orc stared across for a bit. But he had to cross somewhere, and this was the logical time and place. Trumpets blew and the lead cohorts spread to form ranks along the shore. With the next signal, the first rank urged its mounts carefully down the rip-rapped bank and began swimming.

Hovering an oblique six kilometers away, Ivan Yoshida switched the visual pickup from the waiting Northmen to the orcs swimming their horses toward the ambush. When the first rank on their tiring horses had no more than fifty meters farther to swim, arrows began to sleet into it.

After a moment's confusion the line of orcs straightened, still moving forward, the second rank advancing steadily behind them. Three thousand orcs were in the water now. Trumpets blew, and in less than a minute Kamal knew about the ambush. He realized at once what had happened. The Northmen must know the country after all. They had baited him by taking the cattle road, then had swum their horses downstream as they crossed, to land on the north side of the canal after all. He snapped a command. His trumpeter signalled a flanking movement and certain cohorts began letting themselves be carried farther downstream.

Alpha slid through the sky, quartering gravitic

vectors, braked, and flew down the fourth rank of orcs at twenty meters, about eighty meters out from the east bank. Charles alternated short bursts from the two automatic rifles he'd mounted beneath the hull. His Northmen leveled oblique fire from the doors.

The run was completed in seconds, chopping up the third, fourth and fifth ranks. Many of the survivors continued their advance, but some milled in confusion and many others turned their horses downstream. *Alpha* banked and circled for another run. The first two ranks had taken heavier losses to neoviking archery and a few were fighting on the bank. Kniv had platoons of mounted warriors in reserve to hit any bridgehead the orcs might establish.

Meanwhile *Beta* had also entered the action, flying a deadly first run near the west bank. The orcs swimming there broke and turned back, as much because of a screaming siren mounted on the pinnace as the streams of deadly bullets. Troops not yet in the water held back their horses, looking nervously toward their trumpeters.

Ram himself flew the *Beta*. His second run was down the river's midline, siren shrieking again, but he withheld the fire from his mounted guns although his door gunners took their toll. He would be content to break the crossing without maximum kill.

All the swimming ranks began breaking up now in turmoil, trying to get back to the west bank or escape downstream. After his third run, Ram flew to hover seventy meters above the junction of road and river. His voice boomed from the partly raised commast.

"Orcs! Do you surrender? Do you surrender? Dismount, stack your weapons, and line up un-armed, and I will spare your lives." He paused. "Shout your answer! I will hear it!"

There was no immediate answer. Ram glared across at the *Alpha* still moving busily up and down the river killing orcs.

Kamal's aide-de-camp looked worriedly at his commander.

"No!"

"But my Lord, we have no choice! We have no way to fight back!"

"Orcs have never surrendered. Never! I will die first."

As if in answer, *Alpha* skimmed across the water toward them, spewing bullets. The command staff threw themselves from their saddles and embraced the ground among stamping hooves and falling horses. When they got up, those who did, Kamal raised his fist to shake it at the banking *Alpha*, then pitched forward with a dagger between his shoulder blades.

"We surrender!" bellowed his aide-de-camp. "We surrender!"

"Stack your weapons beside the river in big piles," commanded the voice from the sky, "then line up on the road and picket your horses."

Beta floated watchfully as trumpets blew and couriers galloped. *Alpha* was downriver again, kill-ing orcs. Along the banks grew piles of lances, swords and bows. A sluggish stream of mounted orcs flowed onto the road, still disciplined but without their arrogance, finally picketing their horses along the shoulders and forming ranks on foot.

Downstream the short bursts of gunfire from the
Alpha retreated to the edge of hearing. Suddenly
she was back, strafing the long and unarmed ranks
upon the road while fragmentation grenades tumbled from her doors. She made but one run; the orcs
scattered into the marsh grass to flee or hide. Ram
was screaming invective into the radio, spitting
with rage, then shot forward and banked toward
Alpha.

Nils shouted in warning; "*Alpha*! Ta flykk!" *Alpha*
shot into an accelerating climb, and after a moment Ram halted, turned to Nils and poured ob-
scenities on him. When his surge of rage had passed,
he stood panting, face red, eyes bulging.

"You didn't ask my people whether they were
willing to let the orcs surrender," Nils responded
bluntly. "You made *your* peace with them, but you
do not speak for my people. You presumed too
much. To the tribes and many other people, the
orcs are a deadly enemy who would destroy them
if they could and enslave the survivors.

"And how had you intended to deal with your
thousands of prisoners? You have no place to take
them, nothing to feed them, and you could not
control them for long. Your action was without
thought."

Ram glared. "And Ivan!" he said hoarsely, "that
treasonous bastard! He could see what I was doing,
and still he strafed them."

"Why Ivan?" Nils asked. "Sten Vannaren can fly
her and probably did. I told him to make sure he
learned."

"I'll bet you did." Ram fixed him with his eyes.
"I'll bet you were behind the whole rotten treach-
erous thing. Well, that's it, you barbarian filth!

Hostages or no hostages, you'll get no more support from me; no air support and no more ammunition. Absolutely none!"

"Then I'd better explain to Kniv Listi."

The response had been completely matter of fact. Ram hesitated briefly, then reached for the transmitter switch. The exchange in Scandinavian took several minutes, then Nils turned to Ram. "Listi asks no more help from the *Beta*, and will kill no unarmed prisoners in your control as long as they *are* in your control. He retains the right to kill any others. Meanwhile you must bring more ammunition and grenades or he will keep your people."

"But I have *you*!" Ram snapped. "And your woman and brat! You think I won't do anything to you. Don't be too sure."

Nils's mind stared mildly into Ram's, and although the captain usually kept outside thoughts from his consciousness, he felt it opening now to the Northman.

(Ram, Ram, you have become dangerous to yourself. A minute ago you were willing to kill two of your own people; in your rage you didn't care. If you'd killed them, you would have destroyed yourself as well.

(The tribes are not your enemy. They withhold your people because they see your help as the fastest and least costly method of driving the orcs away. Without it, many of my people will die, and many others in other lands.

(So go back to your ship before you do something you will not forgive yourself.)

Ram shivered, feeling physically ill. The word-thoughts flowed on with sure calmness. (The land of the orcs is not the place for you. Ugly things happen here—evil things. Perhaps Chandra and Anne Marie will tell you a little of that someday. Perhaps.

(You are Ram Uithoudt, master artisan, maker of wonders, who sails between the stars. You are not prepared to live with war. Let Matthew Kumalo lead your people down here beneath the sky. He is not as smart as you, but he is wiser, and he has a stronger stomach.)

While the two had faced each other in pregnant silence, the crew had looked on soberly. They had not needed to hear speech to know that something decisive was happening or who was prevailing.

Their captain turned now to the co-pilot.

"Take us back up, Lee," he said quietly, "back to the ship."

When the *Beta* had disappeared, Sten made a run along the bank, spraying the orcs who had crept out of the reeds and tall grass and were rearming themselves from the piles. It was time, he decided, to see if the incendiary grenades could really set the heaps aflame, as Charles had told them.

XXVII

Corporal Sabri had felt it in his bones that today would be different. They'd walked more than forty kilometers yesterday in the trail of the cavalry. Forty kilometers and no sign of the sky chariot that had attacked them in the night, or of Northmen. It was as if they'd been lost track of.

But then, twice in the night mounted men had pounded through the fringes of camp, trampling and slashing. They hadn't been overlooked after all, and he knew that something very bad would happen this day.

So far it hadn't, and the sun was past midday.

The prairie was hilly here. A route along a river would be level but there'd be marshes and meanders to detour, adding miles. If they camped by a marsh it would be harder for horsemen to attack them, or if they camped *in* a marsh. But then they'd be eaten alive by mosquitoes, and it would make little difference to the Northmen anyway. He'd been in the Ukraine; the Northmen always found a way. Masters of trickery, surprise and ambush, they fought head on only when they had to, and then they were the worst of all. Never corner a Northman.

Probably if they captured their women they'd find them all with poison barbs in their loins.

It was heavy work walking uphill through thick knee-high grass, even though the cavalry had ridden it down the day before. Here in the lead rank, locusts rose at their approach, flying jerkily, clicking and buzzing. And increasingly there were flies. The horsemeat they carried was beginning to stink. They'd have been better off to take time to smoke it, if the Northmen weren't going to harass them any more than they had. Probably they were harassing the bastards who still had horses; serve their asses right for riding off like that. Orcs shouldn't ride off like that and leave their buddies. They hadn't even left them any mounted scouts; just abandoned them.

The slope was leveling off, and a trumpet blew the halt. He raised his eyes and looked around. They had climbed a long rounded ridge, affording a view of the previous one behind them and the next one waiting ahead. Above was a vault of pale blue without a speck of cloud to shield them from a baleful sun. And no puff of breeze today, even here on top. Usually there was a breeze, but that too had abandoned them. He wiped sweat from his eyes with a hairy gritty wrist and reached for his canteen.

The murmuring around him changed tone and he looked again toward the west. One of the scouts was approaching, striding steadily toward them against the grade. "What is it?" men called out. "What did you find?"

Sabri couldn't hear his reply, but got it in installments as murmurs crept through the ranks. The cavalry had camped just ahead the night before. There were hundreds of bodies there of men and horses. Served them right, he told himself, the dirty dog robbers.

And there was more to report. The men who'd been left without horses there had not marched on westward; their tracks turned south.

It was a longer break than usual. When the trumpets raised them to their feet again, they too were ordered southward. Any pretense of marching to attack the Northman villages was dead. The idea now was to escape.

The sun was low and they were tired, and impatient to make camp, when the sky chariot came. They stopped, upright and helpless, watching it approach. As it passed overhead, small objects hurtled from it to burst with a roar, and death hissed and warbled. Ranks broke, squads scattering. It circled, swooped, and more of the death stones were hurled at clusters of orcs. The clusters broke, men running singly and in twos and threes and fours, scattering outward, away from each other. The chariot continued to circle low, seeking groups, making loud sharp claps and staccato rattling sounds, and men fell with bleeding holes.

When night came, orcs were scattered over several square kilometers. In the darkness they encountered one another to form small bands. Some moved back to make isolated camps along a creek they'd crossed earlier. Others spent the night where they were. Still others moved on in the darkness seeking safety in maximum separation. No longer were they an army; they were fleeing refugees.

Eight of them were swimming a small river, pushing bundles of reeds that floated their equipment and boots. Helmets and mail had been abandoned; they'd kept only harness, swords and packs. Sabri felt soft mud with his toes, kicked a few strokes farther and waded ashore.

As a horseman he'd been lean; after four days on foot he was leaner. A man could eat rotting horse-meat, but he ate no more than he needed, and maybe less. When all had reached the bank he led them slopping through the tall reeds, carrying his boots. Black muck coated his legs halfway to the knees.

Reeds gave way to waist-high grass, and muck to springy soil. Not far away, carrion birds took flight and he angled toward the spot, the others following. Five orc bodies lay there, just starting to swell. The arrows had frugally been cut out of them and their skulls had been peeled.

It was good, he thought. If Northman searchers had passed through already, perhaps they were safe for a time. The eight sat down, wiped the mud from their feet and ankles with grass, put on their boots, and left.

A trickle of water seeped from the slope. One of them had scooped a hollow with his tough fingers. They were drinking and filling their canteens when they heard the shout from behind. Ten Northmen were on a low rise. They jogged their horses forward, stopping forty meters away with arrows nocked. Boys they were, snot-nosed punks maybe

fifteen or sixteen years old, with the visible beginning of beards on a couple of them.

And they were grinning! Sabri gripped his sword,
a snarl twisting his face, and started toward them,
but for only a few steps before he fell.

XXVIII

The edge of night had passed the Balkans, twilight darkening the Mediterranean as far as Sicily, when *Beta* floated through the gaping portal and settled gently into her cradle. The doors came together slowly and perforce quietly behind her, shutting space outside. Air bled back into the hangar.

When their gages indicated pressure and temperature ship-normal, Willi, Alex, and Nikko got out. Ram was waiting for them, and they walked together toward the briefing room.

"What's the word on Matt?" asked Nikko.

"Jomo says he may have to go in after some tissue and regenerate a new kidney," Ram answered. "He'll know in a day or two. Not that there's any danger—there's not—but I think you'd better stay aboard tomorrow. What'd you find below?"

The quick change of subject did not escape Nikko. He hadn't wanted to give her time to disagree about staying on board.

"Things weren't much different than yesterday," she replied, "but we have a fuller picture now. And a few more magazines of video tape. The Northmen took a prisoner for us—a centurion who speaks

Anglic. Apparently all their officers do. Did. He said the army he was part of was the orc Third Legion. They were supposed to destroy the Northman villages while their warriors were away. A legion is 3,000 men, incidentally. After two nights of air attacks, they were in pretty poor shape, and then the irregular army of mounted farmers and adolescents began hit and run attacks, and finally mop-up operations. He was pretty bitter about *Alpha*—said if it wasn't for her they'd have cleaned out the Northmen. As it was, he doubts that more than a couple hundred mounted orcs reached the forest, and by that time no one knew where anyone else was.

"He got there with a band of six other men, and when he told them they should try to join up with others and find the villages, they refused. Said the only sensible thing to do was get out of the country. He was pretty bitter about that, too."

"How about the men on foot?"

"The same picture as yesterday, only worse. They're scattered all over the prairie, heading south. But they're a lot fewer today. There are whole troops of freeholders and kids on horseback out hunting them. The kids are the worst—hundreds of them, all would-be warriors eager to take an orc scalp while there are any left. And lots of them have, I guess, some of them three or four. Some fifteen- and sixteen-year-olds got carried away with themselves and dismounted, to take on a band of orcs sword to sword. Sten says they didn't do too badly, considering, but several were killed. He seemed to think it was mildly amusing.

"I'll tell you frankly, Ram, I doubt if five dozen

orcs on foot will get out of the country alive, and they'll be the real survivor type."

They went into the narrow conference room and sat around one end of the hardwood table.

"What about the main orc army, that we caught at the river?" Ram asked thoughtfully.

"Most of the survivors must be back in the City by now. We spotted a couple of mounted bands ourselves, riding toward the City from the north. Sten says his people took more than a thousand scalps, and estimates several hundred other orcs must have died in the river, shot from the air or by archers or had their horses killed from under them. With mail shirts on, most that got unhorsed must have drowned; some probably managed to shuck out of them.

"We saw some survivors in the delta country today, too. It looked as if they'd taken over a couple of villages there—as if they weren't even trying to get back to the City. I mentioned it to Sten, thinking he might say something about going to chase them out, but he didn't; I guess to the Northmen the delta fishermen don't mean much."

Ram's eyes were withdrawn. "What do the Northmen plan to do about the City?" he asked.

"I asked him about that. He said they won't attack it in force or besiege it, but they're rounding up the rest of the orc cattle. They also intend to burn the wheat fields when the grain is ripe; he believes they can starve the orcs out. And from a couple of things he said, some raid leaders will probably try to make names for themselves by raiding into the City at night, independently."

"Do you still like the Northmen?"

She did not hesitate. "Yes I do, Ram. They're

friendly honest people, even if they are bloodthirsty and ruthless toward their enemies. I know you're feeling a kind of sympathy for the orcs, but compare the way they treated their hostages with how the Northmen treated me. And consider what the orcs would have done if they'd broken the Northman army."

Ram shook his head without irritation. "It's not a matter of feeling sorry for the orcs," he said quietly. "But each orc is a human being, with one life that's his, and with feelings. And there's the matter of feeling joy in killing, like the Northmen obviously do; that's something I find depraved. From the skimpy picture I've got, partly from you and Charles but partly from Ilse too, an important part of their culture is a set of rules that allows them to enjoy killing their fellow Northmen without destroying their society or suffering from guilt."

"Making a game out of war was an improvement," Nikko answered mildly. "According to tradition, they used to fight each other really ferociously and ruthlessly, tribe against tribe and clan against clan, and really threatened to destroy themselves. Making it a game was progress, not degeneracy."

"They didn't go far enough," Ram said dryly. "They should have written off war altogether. And that's no game they're playing with the orcs." He stopped Nikko's response with a gesture. "Okay, I admit that last wasn't fair; it'd be suicide to play games with the orcs. Did they say when they'll be done with *Alpha*?"

"Sten talked to the chiefs about that. They say we can have it back when they've taken the city."

"Taken the city! Good Lord! That could be months from now!"

Nikko shrugged silently.

"And no assurance we'll get it back then."

"I think we have some assurance," Willi put in. "They've been pretty honest with us so far. Slippery maybe, but they've kept their word. They gave us back all their hostages when you gave them most of our munitions."

Ram grunted, then turning to Nikko he changed the subject. "Do you have all your tapes transferred to the computer?"

"All but today's."

"Good. Matt wants a full session sometime soon, and a full team review of everything that's happened. I want you to start working with Monica tomorrow on a subject retrieval program."

"If I'm doing that, then who'll be in charge of the landing team?"

"I'm going down tomorrow," Ram answered.

"You're not qualified to be in charge," Nikko said.

"I'm going alone."

There was a moment's lag. "Alone?"

He stood, nodding, and turned away from them, walking toward the door. "Alone," he said.

Wordless, they watched him leave. He went to his little office and sat back to think about the day to come.

Sight of a pinnace no longer excited the children, for this was the village of Sten Vannaren, who often landed there. But when the hull went two-way transparent, they stopped to watch, for it held a star man instead of warriors. It settled to the ground, the hydraulic leg-cushions sighed, and the dominant boy of the group trotted off through the morning-wet grass to tell Nils Järnhann.

The Yngling sat cross-legged in the sun outside his tent. It made the boy uncomfortable to have the blind sockets turn toward him as he trotted up, as if there still were eyes in them. All the orcs should die for that, he told himself.

"Nils," he said, "a star man has come in a sky boat."

Nils smiled and rose with easy strength, and the boy moved to take his arm.

"No, I can see."

"Really?" He'd heard what the Yngling seemed to do, but it had not been real to him.

"Really. I wouldn't tease about something like that." He started toward the landing place, the boy hurrying beside him.

Ram sat in the pinnace door, his feet on a step, looking solemnly at the other children, who had come to the foot of the landing steps and were looking back at him. He had spoken to them in Anglic, and they to him in their language, a reflex of the desire to communicate. Neither expected to be understood. A long pause followed each exchange, then either the man or one of the children would speak again.

"This must be a good place to be a child," Ram said. "For two cents I'd take my shoes off and join you."

"Har Du vat å sjutit ijäl orker?"

Pause.

"I'm sorry I can't understand you. I'd like to be your friend though."

The smallest child touched the ladder, then

turned to the one who'd done the talking. "Tror Du å vi få fuga på sjybåten?"

To get a ride in the sky boat! The twelve-year-old eyes turned thoughtful; it hadn't occurred to him. But how to ask?

A heavy shout crossed the meadow, and the children looked across toward a standing warrior figure, then abruptly toward the grove of aspens at which he pointed. A man sat on horseback there, wearing black mail and a plumed helmet. Suddenly the horseman spurred his mount toward the pinnace.

The shout had chilled Ram and he stood, peering toward its source, recognizing the pointing giant despite the hundred-meter separation. The children were scattering like quail.

The shout repeated. "ORC!"

He turned then, saw, and sprang toward the instrument panel to activate the shield, changing intention in mid-stride.

The children!

He snatched a rifle from the rack without taking time to check the magazine, leaped from the door, stumbling as he landed, spun, thumbing the safety, and squeezed the trigger. The gun bucked slightly as 5-millimeter H.V. slugs spurted. The horse plunged heavily and skidded, hurling the orc from the saddle less than twenty meters from the star man. Staggering to his feet, he drew his sword, and Ram squeezed his trigger again.

Then he turned away and vomited.

"Han spyr! Sjäänmannen spyr!" said one of the children [He is vomiting! The star man is vomiting!]

"Jaha," said the twelve-year-old knowingly, "dä sån sjäänfåken visa haten mot orkena." [That's how the star people show their hatred of the orcs.]

Ram rinsed his mouth while waiting for Nils Järnhann, spitting the water into the grass. His hands were shaking and he shoved them in his pockets. The children were examining the dead orc, one lifting the sword from the grass for a clumsy two-handed swing. Ram turned from them and walked to meet the eyeless warrior. Other adults were coming from the encampment now, drawn by the shouts and the shooting.

"Thank you," Nils said, "for saving our children's lives." He paused. "What is it you came to ask?"

"I want to—I think I can get the orcs to leave the country—I hope I can—to leave on their ships and leave their slaves behind. At least I want to try. And I want you along."

Ram sensed that if Nils had had eyes they would be examining him intently, as his mind must be. "Why?" asked the Northman. "Why do you want me along?"

Ram had already asked himself that; asked it in the pinnace as he'd approached the meadow to land. It seemed important to know, but there had been no answer.

"Will you come?"

Nils nodded.

Just then one of the children touched Ram's arm. He looked down. A red-smeared hand held out a crudely hacked scalp to him.

"Dä Din."

"He says it is yours," Nils explained. "It was you who made the kill."

Ram stared. The boy was about twelve, his eyes direct, in attitude resembling a miniature warrior.

Ram took the scalp. "Thank you," he said soberly, and made a slight bow. The boy bobbed in return, then trotted off to where his friends were pulling the mail from the dead torso.

Slowly *Beta* circled the black ㅡower. No one showed themselves despite the voice booming from the commast. *"Orcs! Orcs! I am the commander of the star ship that floats above the sky. I make you an offer. I make you an offer."*

After two minutes no one had appeared. The voice resumed. "I have an offer for the orcs. I offer you your lives. If you refuse, the Northmen will give you death and destruction."

They continued circling; the orcs made no sign. "Why don't they show?" Ram muttered.

"It's a large palace," Nils replied. "Someone would have to take word of us to the commander. He might then want to think for awhile, and after that there are long corridors and stairs to walk. Why don't you talk to them some more? There'll be other interested ears, if not the ruler's."

Ram repeated, waited, repeated again. Moments later three men emerged onto the highest roof garden and stared grimly at the pinnace without speaking. At last one of them called, "I am Dov the Silent. I rule the orcs."

"Here is my offer," Ram's voice boomed. "If the orcs leave their slaves behind and go from this city on their ships, they will not be molested."

The face in the viewscreen was a harsh mask, eyes narrowed, mouth a gash. "Why should we do that? We need our slaves to do for us, and we are a great army. The Northmen cannot dig us out of here, although we hope they try."

Nils reached out his hand, and after a moment's hesitation Ram gave him the microphone.

"Orc, I am Ironhand, the Northman who killed a lion and a strutting coward in your arena, blasted the throng through the troll's mind, and escaped. Who killed Kazi with my sword. Captured and blinded, I escaped your dungeon and led my warriors into the bowels of the palace to take your hostages from you.

"So listen to me. You are bunglers. Your brave words are hollow, like your soldiers. Your people have fought Northmen time and again, with great advantage of numbers; you have never won. Your soldiers know they cannot beat us.

"Each time we've fought, you've been weakened. Where are the thirty-five thousand you boasted of a year ago? Thousands are bleached bones in the Ukraine. In one day you shrank by half, when the horse barbarians abandoned you as men already doomed.

"Ten days ago ten thousand orcs rode out to destroy us, with a sky chariot to help them. Today we have the sky chariot. We took eleven hundred scalps near the river, and even close to your city. Hundreds of orcs feed the fish. Flies blow in the corpses of the Third Legion; not three hundred of them are alive, little bands of fleeing men hiding by day and skulking southward by night. They do not take ten steps without looking backward."

Ram stared at the blind barbarian with something like awe. What a speaker, and in a language not his own!

"And ruler, where are yesterday's rulers? Kazi, who lived many lifetimes, dead by my sword. And what became of the strutting Draco when he flew out to destroy the Northmen?

"You defy us to dig you out of your city. Why

should we trouble to? Can the orcs eat stone. Where are your cattle? Who guards your grain fields now that the Northmen fly abroad in the sky? Your horses swell and stink in their paddocks since our sky chariot visited them; they feed the worms. Will you eat your slaves then? They won't last long. Then you will have to eat each other.

"Listen to the star man, orc. He is a rare one, a man who does not want to see the orcs all dead."

The orc shouted back, his voice hoarse, defiant. "Then why does a Northman speak for him? If the Northmen can starve us out, then why do you, a Northman, want to let us leave freely and unmolested? Because you're afraid of us after all! We are still the orcs, mighty and great in numbers!"

"Afraid of you after all what? After all your defeats?" Nils's voice was bored now. "No, there is nothing there to fear. We'll be rid of you one way or another, and the Northmen owe the star men a favor. So the captain of the star men has claimed the right to save your lives if you will depart and leave your slaves behind."

"How do we know you won't fly down and attack us on our ships?"

"You have only our oath; you take a chance. But if you stay, you face a certainty: cannibalism, starvation, and death."

The orc stood sullenly, both aides talking to him at once. He snarled and they backed away; then he looked up at the pinnace again and shouted in Anglic:

"Kazi said it to our fathers! 'This will be the place of the orcs as long as the tower shall stand!' The Master's spirit will strengthen and save us! He *is* undying!"

At that moment Ram knew what to do. Siren shrieking, he twice swung *Beta* around the tower as he lifted away. As he rose even with its top, he cut off the siren and answered Dov the Silent, the commast speaker on full volume now. The words rolled like small thunder over the palace.

"AS LONG AS THE TOWER SHALL STAND? THEN THE TOWER WILL FALL!"

The night was clear and moonless, with a chill breeze. Mikhail Ciano led the task force—men in asbestos suits and oxygen masks. Orcs shivering on roof tops stared fearfully at the grotesque forms at the base of the tower, at the beams of laser drills and the glow of molten rock. The snorkel worked ceaselessly at handling the heat that built up within the shield. At intervals, when the build-up became excessive, the shield was switched off for a moment to let the night wind blow the heat away. Finally the glow died, and shortly the shield switched off again. There was a series of small explosions as coolant was jetted into bore holes; then the shield was reactivated and all was quiet. At last the pinnace lifted and disappeared into the night sky.

Nothing happened. The soldiers, who had watched almost without speaking, began talking softly among themselves, and a few started leaving the roofs. Abruptly a stupendous roar shook the night as great gouts of flame shot from the base of the tower. Its dim bulk seemed to lean, did lean, like a colossal tree whose roots had rotted, fell with a stupefying shock of sound across the roof gardens, caving in whole sections of the palace, and rumbled into the square below.

The death of its echoes left silence and deafness for long seconds, while orcs rose first to knees and elbows, then trembling to their feet on nearby roofs. A single voice began to wail, was joined by another, growing to a chorus that thickened the night.

XXIX

But if on Earth mankind had died,
Satan lived there still,
Like Onan cast his seed beside that sea
as dragon's teeth,
and up there sprang
orcs.

Nursed on battered breasts
to monsters grew,
their arrogance,
swollen with sadism,
sustained by screams,
restored through massacre.

In such a universe
how can I live?
And yet unhumaned
do not die,
memories like maggots
crawling through my damaged brain.

From—EARTH, by Chandra Queiros

There was defeat in Dov's face, in his voice and his manner, although his back was still straight. All slaves would remain in the City except skilled seamen to work the sheets and lines. Orcs themselves would row.

The exodus began early the morning following the agreement. *Beta* hovered within sight of those below, shifting now and then. All day formations of orcs marched to the harbor, boarded galleys and left. The team watching from the pinnace was impressed with their order, the sharp rectangularity of their units.

And there was no sign of cheating, no hint that slaves were being smuggled in orc garb. None among the marchers lacked the ramrod spine, the erect head, the quick strong in-step stride of an orc. Or the sword. Without exception all were orcs, remarkably rehabilitated after all their defeats.

Nor had any slaves been smuggled to the harbor in the night; the IR scanner vouched for that. Besides, the galleys were open, undecked except for forecastle and poop; there was little room for concealment.

Apparently the threat of embargo and starvation had set deep hooks in the orc chief's mind, and he probably knew of the monitoring ability which the pinnaces had.

By nightfall only a few hulls remained in the harbor. The rest were strung out over many kilometers of sea, running near the shore and working southward. By morning many would be passing the wooded coast of what once had been Bulgaria. The *Beta's* crew stood solitary introspective watches through the night. With the sun the same few hulls were still empty beside the docks.

"That's right, Captain," Mikhail said into the radio. "Apparently they're either excess or not seaworthy. I suspect it's the latter; the orcs seemed pretty crowded on those they sailed in.

"No, we're all pretty sure they didn't take any slaves with them except for about six per ship as agreed on. We used a magnification that gave us a good look at them: typical lovable orcs, arrogant in spite of all. Pretty remarkable, considering. We got a good count, too; about seventy-three hundred in perfect military order. Just about as many as we calculated there should be."

They exchanged a few listless comments then and broke communication. *Beta* hung tiresomely at three kilometers through the long sunny morning and past midday, watching. The city below seemed dead. They were not sure whether their vigil was over or there was more to watch for. Mikhail considered suggesting they ask the Northmen to land a patrol, but decided to wait.

Charles stared narrowly at the screen.

"Mike?"

"Yeah?"

"There's something fishy down there."

"I know. The Black Sea."

Charles glanced at him with irritation. "Why don't we see any slaves?"

Mikhail didn't answer, but his expression changed.

"There out to be thousands of them moving around down there," Charles went on. "Celebrating or something. I haven't seen more than a handful."

They looked at one another, the thought shaping itself in both their minds. Mikhail reached for the controls and the pinnace began to drop; all of them were alert now. Briefly they circled the palace at a hundred meters, then settled toward the rubble-heaped square.

"Me and Ivan," Charles said, "if it's all right with him."

Ivan nodded, patting the grenade-filled pocket that bulged on his right thigh.

"Okay," said Mikhail, "but be careful. We'll try to cover you if there's any need."

The snorkel sucked it in as they lowered farther, and they smelled it strongly when they opened the door. Charles and Ivan, pistols in hand, started toward the nearest building, and the *Beta* rose to ten meters, ready. The two disappeared through a doorway, emerged two minutes later and did not call to the pinnace. They checked two more buildings before stopping in an intersection and signaling. The *Beta* landed again.

"They left 'em behind, all right." Charles' face was an improbable gray. "The ones we saw moving around must have found hiding places and come out afterwards. Massacre must have been night before last; the maggots have hatched already."

"Are you going to tell Ram?" Ivan asked quietly.

"I'll have to," Mikhail replied.

"Can he take it?"

"I hope so. He's had a better grip on himself lately—the last few days."

Ivan continued to look at him, his eyes sober. Mikhail reached for the radio switch. "Wish me luck."

XXX

There were nineteen people in the narrow conference room, with Matthew and Ram at one end of the table. Ram had said little, and Matthew presided in his usual style, loosely.

Carlos Lao was enjoying the adversary role. "Use a little vision, Nikko. They have a whole city open to them. Other tribes, in Earth's old history, became civilized in a single generation when they moved into a conquered city and began living there."

"Come on now, Carl," said Alex Malaluan, "you don't seriously think it was the buildings and streets of Rome that civilized the conquering Visigoths, do you? It was the Romans themselves."

"What makes you think the fifth-century Romans were any more civilized than the Visigoths who conquered them?" Nikko asked.

Alex persisted. "And the Northmen would be moving into an empty city. What sort of skills and manpower would it take to keep it operating? To keep water flowing in the ducts? Keep sewers repaired and functioning, provide labor and the transportation of goods? Warriors and hunters and

239

herdsmen don't know how to do those things, and they're probably not inclined to learn. Slaves were the engineers and accountants and laborers, and almost all of them are dead. When they died, the city died; those buildings are the bones."

Carlos sighed noisily. "All right, I was wrong. And anyway," he added, smirking at Nikko, "the Northmen would have to be flexible, willing to change, even if the slaves were still available."

"And?"

"And according to you, they have their poet laureate writing an epic hymn celebrating the victory of the Northmen and their way of life over the corrupt orcs."

"They *are* willing to change though," Nikko corrected. "They have changed, and are changing. Fifteen months ago they were forest dwellers in Scandinavia who rode horses rather little and not very skillfully. They didn't even have a word for prairie or steppe—didn't even know there was such a thing. They've settled for calling it storäng, great meadow. They were an assortment of clans and tribes raiding and feuding with one another. Now they're united—even refer to themselves collectively as *the People*—and in less than a year's time they turned themselves into first-rate cavalry.

"But in a sense you're right. They do resist change in what they consider cultural basics. They still believe that life as herdsmen and farmers, hunters and warriors, is best for personal and cultural health and vigor. Their changes amount to adjusting their old life-ways to new circumstances and a new physical environment, without changing their principles.

"I'm not sure how smooth and easy it will be for them. They're getting ready now to explore the foothills and mountains all around the prairie, all the way around to northern Bulgaria. They're a people used to lots of room, who've been crowded together for months. They'll need to decide on new clan and tribal territories.

"And a tougher job will be to decide on whether and how to change the laws governing feuds and wars among themselves. A lot of them feel they shouldn't raid each other like they used to. They feel a lot closer to each other since they first met the orcs, and lots of them feel there are plenty of outsiders they can fight. But others feel that outsiders are too easy, that real warrior merit can be earned only by fighting worthy opponents—namely other Northmen. They'd fight outsiders only from necessity.

"And of course there's the likelihood that if they fight other people too much, the others will pick up Northman tactics and methods of training and so forth and become a lot more dangerous."

Alex raised an eyebrow. "That last bit of reasoning sounds pretty sophisticated," he said. "Are you sure you didn't think of it yourself? It doesn't strike me as a product of the barbarian mind."

"No, I heard it down there, although I have to admit it was Nils who mentioned it. But there were primitives long ago who were fairly sophisticated in some respects, and we also need to keep in mind that these people may have carried down certain concepts and attitudes from the civilized past.

"At any rate they discuss their problems quite openly; it's a remarkably open society. Even when I was a hostage they let me wander around camp freely. I talked to whoever didn't seem too busy, and most of them were happy to visit with that naive and curious star woman. I learned to handle twenty-ninth century Scandinavian pretty well, too. The major changes have been simplifications. For example they've dropped the neuter gender, changed the past tense of almost . . ."

"Whoa, stop! Enough!" Matt said. "No linguistic analyses." He looked down the two lines of familiar faces for a moment before continuing. "Ram told me before we came in that one of the things we need to talk about is when we're going to start home, and this is a good time to get into that. Ram?"

Ram leaned back in his chair. "I'll let Jomo tell you what he told me," the captain said quietly. "He's got the major reasons for a prompt departure."

The chief medical officer stood up. "Anne Marie and Chandra need treatment we can't give them here. Especially Chan. All we can do on the *Phaeacia* is keep him alive, and I'm not sure we can do that for very long. Somewhere within that coma there seems to be a profound wish, or willingness at least, to die; his physical injuries are not actually severe. We need to start for home as soon as we can."

"Not *we*, Jomo," Matthew said. "Chan and Anne. And all they need to take them there is the ship and crew. The exploration team came here to learn, and most of us have hardly set foot on Earth.

"With a landing grid waiting back home, you don't need the pinnaces; they can stay here with us. Nikko wants to spend more time with the Northmen, and I can base my operations with them. She swears that Big Nils is a new kind of human being, maybe a major new step in human evolution. Incidentally, did you know he's only twenty-one years old? And there are the Psi Kinfolk that Ilse sprang from—a whole culture of telepaths scattered throughout central and western Europe."

"The Kinfolk would really be interesting," Celia broke in. "I wish I could stay and study them myself. From what Ilse told me, they must be a living repository of post-plague history and political lore."

"And there are the orcs," Nikko added. "Some of the surviving slaves are educated people, and one of Kazi's daughters is with them. There'll be a lot we can learn about the orcs from them, and especially from her.

"Nils insists that Kazi was born before the plague and was one continuous personality, one unbroken ego-memory sequence—he terms it 'one being' —reincarnated time after time by taking over selected bodies. It sounds preposterous, but it would explain some of the things about orc culture, including the name *orc* and the black tower of the palace, both right out of the old twentieth-century fantasy classic, *Lord of the Rings*. And last night I found corroboration of sorts in the history bank. There was a *Timur Karim Kazi* born in 2064, Earth Reckoning, in Kabul, Afghanistan—a neurophysiologist and professor of Psionics, of which there probably weren't more than a few dozen on the planet. He was something of a genius."

"We hoped there'd be a lot to learn here," Matthew put in. "Now we're beginning to appreciate *how much* there is. That ingrown little culture of ours is in for one heck of a shot of ideas."

Ram looked rueful. "That was Gus's idea in pushing this project for so long, God rest him. Then, when we got here, too much happened too fast.

"And one thing about leaving you behind—when we get home, they'll have to let us come back here. It makes an ongoing operation out of it, not an abortion.

"One other thing: Jomo and Cele agree that an optical transplant should be possible for Nils, back home, although apparently it would be more cosmetic than anything else. He is definitely able to see without eyes. But we can take him with us, if he'd like."

Three days later the *Phaeacia's* mass-proximity drive winked, sending her on the first phase of her trip back to New Home—their real home, their own culture, not a home of ancient history and sentiment. While the *Alpha* and *Beta* rode down into the troposphere on a gravitic vector through the Northmen's encampment.

XXXI

(From an interview with Professor Nikko Kumalo on the occasion of her ninetieth birthday.)

You might have thought that experiences like those we'd gone through would have made us more cautious, even frightened us off. But it didn't work that way. The orcs had been our great *bête noir*—Draco our Gog and orcdom our Magog so to speak—and the orcs had been broken and we were disengaged from them. Thanks to the Neovikings and that remarkable young man they called their Youngling.

Oh, we all realized there were other hazards as deadly as the orcs, if somewhat less horrible: brigand bands and horse barbarians and feudal lords, as well as others we presumed must exist but didn't know about. But we committed ourselves to stay.

Now I don't want you to imagine we were being brave and noble in the service of science or man. It was more a sense of adventure and destiny and something like innocence. It seemed like the only thing to do. So we turned and went back down, with no real misgivings or fear. We were still somehow eager to learn more, and for experiences that would make us feel even more alive, albeit at some risk of becoming dead. You have to remember that our engineered and programmed agrarian democracy had become deadly dull for people with the life and spirit needed to get into that first space program.

I mentioned a sense of destiny. That was part of it. And the feeling wasn't just mine, or something an old woman has added to the rememberings of her youth. We've all reminisced on it together many times, those of us who could.

It's good that we did go back, of course, despite the cost. Our world and our future would be quite different if we hadn't—much less interesting. Much less promising. But even so, it's well that we don't know our future, or at least not clearly or with any certainty. First of all it wouldn't be much fun that way. And secondly—no, there isn't any secondly. It just wouldn't be much fun. That's why people like change and resent those who try to prevent it. To a large degree, quality of life is a function of not knowing what will happen, of trying to influence it, and experiencing some amount of success.

That, young man, is what makes a rich life: uncertainty, and anticipation, and succeeding when it counts most. But some people simply can't tolerate much richness. I can, and I've had a fine full share of it. The only person I've ever envied is Nils Järnhann, not for his marvelous talents but for what he would eventually undertake.